The Tales of Uncle Remus

The Adventures of Brer Rabbit

as told by JULIUS LESTER

illustrated by Jerry Pinkney

PUFFIN BOOKS

PUFFIN BOOKS
Published by the Penguin Group
Penguin Putnam Books for Young Readers, 345 Hudson Street, New York, New York 10014, U.S.A.
Penguin Books Ltd, 27 Wrights Lane, London W8 5TZ, England
Penguin Books Australia Ltd, Ringwood, Victoria, Australia
Penguin Books Canada Ltd, 10 Alcorn Avenue, Toronto, Ontario, Canada M4V 3B2
Penguin Books (N.Z.) Ltd, 182-190 Wairau Road, Auckland 10, New Zealand

Penguin Books Ltd, Registered Offices: Harmondsworth, Middlesex, England

First published in the United States of America by Dial Books, a division of Penguin Books USA Inc., 1987
Published by Puffin Books, a member of Penguin Putnam Books for Young Readers, 1999

10 9 8 7 6 5 4

Design by Jane Byers Bierhorst

THE LIBRARY OF CONGRESS HAS CATALOGED THE DIAL EDITION AS FOLLOWS:
Lester, Julius.
The tales of Uncle Remus.
Contents: The adventures of Brer Rabbit.
1. Afro-Americans—Folklore. 2. Tales—United States.
[1. Folklore, Afro-American. 2. Animals—Fiction.]
I. Jerry Pinkney, ill. II. Title.
PZ8.1.L434Tal 1987 [398.2] 85-20449
ISBN 0-8037-0271-X
ISBN 0-8037-0272-8 (lib. bdg.)

Puffin ISBN 0-14-130347-6

The publisher wishes to express its sincere thanks to the estate of Joel Chandler Harris
for its gracious support during the publication of this new version of *The Tales of Uncle Remus.*

*Each black-and-white drawing is made of pencil and graphite; each full-color picture consists
of a pencil, graphite, and watercolor painting that is color-separated and reproduced in full color.*

Printed in Hong Kong

To the memory of my father
J. L.

For my children,
Troy, Brian, Scott, and Myles
J. P.

My lasting memories of my grandmother are of her telling me stories. I know that she told folktales and fairy tales from many parts of the world. I cried when she told Andersen's "Little Match Girl"—it was so beautiful and so sad. But my favorites, and I'm sure they were hers as well, were the Brer Rabbit stories. I howled with laughter when Brer Rabbit asked the Tar Baby "and how does your symptoms segashuate?" My grandmother did not attempt to use the dialect of Joel Chandler Harris because, even though she had been born on a Maryland plantation in 1862, she did not speak the way Harris interpreted slave speech. Her mother had told her the stories and she told them to me with love and affection as she sat in her favorite rocking chair in the middle of a large, old-fashioned kitchen. It was a way for her to entertain me as she watched her cooking.

In 1917 when I was old enough to go to school I still wanted to hear about Brer Rabbit and Miz Meadows and the gals, so I would rush home to be there by "pot-watching" time. "Grandma," I'd ask, "tell about how Brer Rabbit tricked Brer Fox." We would get comfortable and start down Brer Rabbit's road. Small, helpless Brer Rabbit always defeated his adversaries—the large animals—with his wit, humor, and wisdom. In my smallness I related to the clever little hare who could always get out of the most difficult situations through his sharp wit.

I soon wanted to read these stories myself, which led me to

the only collections available, by Joel Chandler Harris. They were in a dialect that was like a foreign language and I could not handle it. I was frustrated and, although I loved the stories, I was too impatient to struggle with the words. Grandmother died and the Brer Rabbit stories were put into the storage of my mind.

It wasn't until several years later, in college, that I learned about the importance of these stories as true American folklore. Dr. Harold Thompson, a leading American folklorist, gave a lecture on people from the West Coast of Africa who had been captured and sold as slaves. Some were settled in the southern states where they took stories from home about a hare—Wakaima—and adapted them to their new surroundings. Wakaima became Brer Rabbit and the clay man became the Tar Baby. Learning about this made me turn to the books again, and once again I tried unsuccessfully to read them.

In 1937 I found myself in the 135th Street branch of the New York Public Library located in the heart of Harlem as a children's librarian. One of the prerequisites of this position was to tell stories. I soon learned that these black boys and girls needed to be introduced to the humor and hidden philosophies of Brer Rabbit and his cohorts. Here was a contribution to their racial pride—to know that their black forefathers had first told these stories and, in so doing, had added to the body of American folklore. Many of them were sensitive to the slave setting that showed Uncle Remus telling the stories to the little white boy, so I eliminated that frame. It became obvious that the tales stood on their own as their African counterparts about Wakaima did.

One day a young, dynamic woman came to the children's room and told me that she was a student in Lucy Sprague Mitchell's Bank Street writing course. She had decided that her project would be to retell the Uncle Remus stories. Her name was Margaret Wise Brown, who later became an outstanding author of books for the very young. She too realized that the stories could be removed from their slave setting without losing any of their unique qualities. So she eliminated the figure of Uncle Remus and titled her project simply "Brer Rabbit" and subsequently had it published under the same title. But she retained the phrasing and speech patterns of Joel Chandler Harris because she did not have the rhythm and natural speech patterns of the southern blacks. A true translation and interpretation would come from within the black experience.

Despite the drawbacks in Harris's text, I still loved the stories and appreciated Brer Rabbit as a cultural hero and a significant part of my heritage. However, I was telling the stories less and less often because of the dialect. Then in the late forties and early fifties the Harlem schools along with others with liberal philosophies in New York City were asking that their classes be given lectures on black history. How could I represent our African background and the relationship between Africa and black America to primary grades? How could I show the fusion of the different African cultures and the cultures existing in America and the West Indies?

The answer came one day as I was planning a story hour. I would tell "Wakaima and the Clay Man," discuss in simple terms the middle passage (the slaves' experiences on slave ships), relate Wakaima to Brer Rabbit, and finally tell "Brer Rabbit and the Tar Baby." Once again I would be telling the animal stories without a truly satisfactory book for the children. As a librarian and one who feels that storytelling is an ideal way to bring together children and books, my frustration grew.

In 1972 a book was placed on my desk and I knew immediately that I had found the answer to years of seeking. Julius Lester had written *The Knee-High Man and Other Tales*, published by Dial. Here were black folktales told perfectly. Lester had used the voice and the language of black people. And he does so again in his tellings of the Uncle Remus stories. In the foreword to this book he calls it "a modified contemporary southern black English, a combination of standard English and black English where sound is as important as meaning." He has preserved the story lines, the wit, the humor—all of the attributes which have made the stories so much a part of my life—while making them accessible to readers. It is interesting to read the foreword to this collection, preferably before reading the stories. Much research and personal feeling have been distilled into a concise, historical, and chronological explanation of the Uncle Remus stories. This foreword is invaluable to the appreciation of the tales.

I can not emphasize enough the importance of telling the stories. As you listen to yourself the rhythm and melodic language of Lester's telling will come forth. The contemporary approach to some of the stories brings them into today's lifestyle. They fit into the traditional and bring a modern humor to the stories. They must be told and I look forward to sharing them with children.

Augusta Baker

Columbia, South Carolina
August 1985

Augusta Baker is former Coordinator of Children's Services of
The New York Public Library and Storyteller-in-Residence
at the University of South Carolina.

Contents

How the Animals Came to Earth

Most folks don't know it, but the animals didn't always live on earth. Way back before "In the beginning" and "Once upon a time," they lived next door to the Moon. They'd probably still be there if Brer Rabbit and Sister Moon hadn't started squabbling with one another like they were married. The way it come about was like this:

The animals liked to sit out in their yards every evening and look at Sister Moon. They thought she was just about the prettiest thing they'd ever seen, and Sister Moon never argued with them. Well, the animals started noticing that she was losing weight. To tell the truth, she was looking downright puny, like she had gone on a cottage cheese diet.

Brer Rabbit decided to climb over the fence to find out what was going on. "What's the matter, Sister Moon? I don't mean to hurt your feelings or nothing like that, but you look po' as Job's turkey."

Sister Moon said, "I ain't been feeling like myself of late."

"Is there anything I can do to help you?"

"Thank you, Brer Rabbit, but I don't believe you the man to do what I need doing."

Brer Rabbit was insulted. "I'm more man than Brer Sun who you chase all over the sky every month and can't catch up to."

Sister Moon smiled tightly. "All right, Brer Rabbit. I'll try you out. I need to get word to Mr. Man that I ain't feeling like myself. I believe I done caught cold from being out in the night air so much. If I don't put my light out and take a little vacation, I'm going to be in a bad way. I don't want Mr. Man to look up and see my light out one night and get scared."

"I'll take the word to him. I been wanting to see what a something called Mr. Man look like anyway."

"Tell Mr. Man I said, 'I'm getting weak for to be more strong. I'm going in the shade for to get more light.'"

Brer Rabbit said it over a couple of times and off he went.

He took a running start and jumped a long jump. He fell through space, past the stars and down through the firmament, tumbling tail over head and head over behind. This was no place for a rabbit! He was so scared, his eyes got big and wide and almost popped out of his head and they been that way ever since. This was the last time his mouth was going to get him into something his feet couldn't do.

He landed on Earth and waited a few minutes to make sure he had all his parts and they were in working order. Then he looked around. The first thing he saw was Mr. Man's garden. It was filled with green peas, lettuce, cabbage, collard greens, and sparrow grass. Over in the field were sheep, cows, goats, and pigs. Brer Rabbit's mouth started trembling and dribbling at the same time.

He went up to Mr. Man's house, knocked on the door, and said, "I got a message for you from Sister Moon."

"What is it?"

Brer Rabbit thought for a minute. "She say, 'I'm getting weak; I got no strength. I'm going to where the shadows stay.' "

Mr. Man got indignant. "Tell Sister Moon I said, 'Seldom seen and soon forgot; when Sister Moon dies her feet get cold.' "

Brer Rabbit nodded and took a long jump back up to Sister Moon. He told her what Mr. Man said. Sister Moon was angry. She hauled off and hit Brer Rabbit with a shovel and split his lip. Brer Rabbit don't take no stuff off nobody and he clawed and scratched Sister Moon. And to this day you can seek the marks—rabbits have split lips and the face of the moon is all scratched up and got holes in it.

Brer Rabbit went and told the animals about all the vegetables and sheep and goats and fat pigs he'd seen on Mr. Man's place. They decided right then that Sister Moon was on her own from now on.

They took the long jump and this is where they've been ever since.

How Brer Fox and Brer Dog Became Enemies

When the animals started living here on Earth, something seemed to happen to them. Where before they had gotten along with each other, now they started having little arguments and disagreements. It was only a matter of time before they weren't much different from people.

Brer Fox and Brer Rabbit were sitting alongside the road one day talking about much of nothing when they heard a strange sound—*blim, blim, blim.*

"What's that?" Brer Fox wanted to know. He didn't know whether to get scared or not.

"That?" answered Brer Rabbit. "Sound like Sister Goose."

"What she be doing?"

"Battling clothes," said Brer Rabbit.

I know y'all don't know what I'm talking about. You take your clothes to the Laundromat, or have a washing machine and dryer sitting right in the house. Way back yonder folks took their clothes down to the creek or stream or what'nsoever, got them real wet, laid'em across a big rock or something, took a stick and *beat* the dirt out of them. You don't know nothing about no clean clothes until you put on some what been cleaned with a battlin' stick.

Well, when Brer Fox heard that Sister Goose was down at the stream, his eyes got big and Brer Rabbit knew his mind had just gotten fixed on supper. Brer Fox said he reckoned he better be getting home. Brer Rabbit said he supposed he should do the same, and they went their separate ways.

Brer Rabbit doubled back, however, and went down to the stream where Sister Goose was.

"How you today, Sister Goose?"

"Just fine, Brer Rabbit. Excuse me for not shaking hands with you, but I got all these suds on my hands."

Brer Rabbit said he understood.

I suppose I got to stop the story, 'cause I can hear you thinking that a goose don't have hands. And next thing I know you be trying to get me to believe that snakes don't have feet and cats don't have wings, and I know better! So, if you don't mind, you can keep your thoughts to yourself and I'll get back to the story.

After Brer Rabbit and Sister Goose had finished exchanging the pleasantries of the day, Brer Rabbit said, "I got to talk with you about Brer Fox. He's coming for you, Sister Goose, and it'll probably be before daybreak."

Sister Goose got all nervous and scared. "What am I gon' do, Brer Rabbit? My husband is dead and ain't no man around the house. What am I gon' do?"

Brer Rabbit thought for a minute. "Take all your clothes and roll 'em up in a nice clean white sheet and put that on your bed tonight. Then you go spend the night up in the rafters."

So, that's what Sister Goose did. But she also sent for her friend, Brer Dog, and asked him if he'd keep watch that night. He said he'd be glad to.

Just before daybreak Brer Fox creeped up to the house, looked around, eased the front door open and slipped inside. He saw something big and white on the bed. He grabbed it and ran out the door. Soon as he jumped off the porch, Brer Dog came out from under the house growling and scratching up dirt. Brer Fox dropped that bundle of clothes like it was a burning log and took off! It's a good thing, too, 'cause it had taken Brer Dog four months to find somebody who could wash and iron his pajamas as good as Sister Goose, and he wasn't about to let nothing happen to her.

Next day when the news got around that Brer Fox had tried to steal Sister Goose's laundry, he couldn't go nowhere for a week. Brer Fox blamed Brer Dog for spreading the news through the community, and ever since that day, the Dog and the Fox haven't gotten along with each other.

"Hold'im Down, Brer Fox"

Brer Fox couldn't prove it, but he knew Brer Rabbit had warned Sister Goose he was coming, and he made up his mind to get even. Brer Rabbit got word about what Brer Fox was thinking on, so he stayed away from his regular habitats for a while.

On this particular day he was somewhere up around Lost Forty and saw a great big Horse laying dead out in a pasture. Or he thought it was dead until he saw the Horse's tail switch.

Brer Rabbit went on his way, but who should he see coming toward him but Brer Fox!

"Brer Fox! Brer Fox! Come here! Quick! I got some good news! Come here!"

Brer Fox didn't care what kind of good news Brer Rabbit had. The good news was that he had found that rabbit! Just as Brer Fox got in grabbing distance, Brer Rabbit said:

"Come on, Brer Fox! I done found how we can have enough fresh meat to last us until the middle of next Septerrary."

Brer Fox, being a prudent man, thought he should check this out. "What you talking about, Brer Rabbit?"

"I just found a Horse laying on the ground where we can catch him and tie him up."

Sounded good to Brer Fox. "Let's go!"

Brer Rabbit led him over to the pasture, and sho' nuf', there was the Horse laying on the ground like he was waiting for them. Brer Rabbit and Brer Fox got to talking about how to tie him up. They argued back and forth for a while until finally Brer Rabbit said:

"Listen. I tell you the way we do it. I'll tie you to his tail and when he tries to get up, you can hold him down. If I was a big strong man like you, I'd do it, and you know, if I was to hold him, he would be held. But I ain't got your strength. Of course, if you scared to do it, then I reckon we got to come up with another plan."

There was something about the plan that Brer Fox didn't like, but he couldn't think of what it was. Not wanting Brer Rabbit to think he wasn't strong and brave, he said O.K.

Brer Rabbit tied him to the Horse's tail. "Brer Fox! That Horse don't know it, but he caught!" Brer Fox grinned weakly.

Brer Rabbit got him a great, long switch and hit the Horse on the rump—POW! The Horse jumped up and landed on his feet and there was Brer Fox, dangling upside down in the air, too far off the ground for peace of mind.

"Hold'im down, Brer Fox! Hold'im down!"

The Horse felt something on his tail. He started jumping and raring and bucking and Brer Fox knew now what was wrong with Brer Rabbit's idea.

"Hold'im down, Brer Fox! Hold'im down!"

The Horse jumped and twirled and snorted and bucked, but Brer Fox hung on.

"Hold'im down, Brer Fox! Hold'im down!"

One time Brer Fox managed to shout back, "If I got *him* down, who got hold of *me*?"

But Brer Rabbit just yelled, "Hold'im down, Brer Fox! You got him now! Hold'im down!"

The Horse started kicking with his hind legs and Brer Fox slid down the tail. The Horse kicked him in the stomach once, twice, three times, and Brer Fox went sailing through the air. It was a week and four days before Brer Fox finally come to earth, which gave him a whole lot of time to realize that Brer Rabbit had bested him again.

Brer Rabbit Comes to Dinner

It took Brer Fox a while to recuperate, but that gave him a lot of time to scheme and plan on how he was going to get Brer Rabbit.

The very first day Brer Fox was up and about, he sauntered down the road. Coming toward him looking as plump and fat as a Christmas turkey was Brer Rabbit.

"Just a minute there!" Brer Fox said as Brer Rabbit started to walk past without speaking.

"I'm busy," said Brer Rabbit. "I'm full of fleas today and got to go to town and get some ointment."

"This won't take more than a minute," Brer Fox answered, falling into step beside him.

"All right. What's on your mind?"

Brer Fox gave a sheepish grin. "Well, Brer Rabbit. I saw Brer Bear yesterday and he said I ought to make friends with you. I felt so bad when he finished with me that I promised I'd make up with you the first chance I got."

Brer Rabbit scratched his head real slow like. "Awright, Brer Fox. I believe Brer Bear got a point. To show you I mean business, why don't you drop over to the house tomorrow and take supper with me and the family?"

Next day Brer Rabbit helped his wife fix up a big meal of cabbages, roasting ears, and sparrow grass. Long about supper time the children came in the house all excited, hollering, "Here come Brer Fox!"

Brer Rabbit told them to sit down to the table, mind their manners, and be quiet. He wanted everything to be just right. So everybody sat down and waited for Brer Fox to knock on the door. They waited a long time, but no knock came.

"Are you sure that was Brer Fox you saw coming up the road?" he asked his children.

"We sure. He was drooling at the mouth."

No mistake. That was Brer Fox.

Brer Rabbit got out of his chair very quietly and cracked the door open. He peeped one of his eyeballs out. He rolled his eyeballs from one side of the yard to the other until they stopped on a bush that looked like it was growing a fox's tail. Fox's tail! Brer Rabbit slammed the door real quick.

Next day Brer Fox sent word by Brer Mink that he had been low-down sick the day before and was sorry he couldn't come. To make up for it, he'd sho' be pleased if Brer Rabbit would take supper with him that very same evening.

When the shadows were at their shortest, Brer Rabbit went over to Brer Fox's. He'd scarcely set one foot on the porch when he heard groaning from inside. He opened the door and saw Brer Fox sitting in his rocking chair, a blanket over his shoulder, looking like Death eating soda crackers in the graveyard. Brer Rabbit looked around and didn't see any supper on the stove. He did notice the butcher knife and roasting pan on the counter, however.

"Looks like you planning on us having chicken for supper, Brer Fox," says Brer Rabbit like nothing was wrong.

"Sho' nuf'," says Brer Fox.

"You know what goes good with chicken, Brer Fox?"

"What's that?"

"Calamus root! Seems like I can't eat chicken no other way nowadays." And before Brer Fox could blink, Brer Rabbit was out the door and into the bushes where he hid to see if Brer Fox was sho' nuf' sick.

A minute later Brer Fox come out on the porch looking as healthy as a rat in a tuxedo. Brer Rabbit stuck his head out of the bushes and said, "I leave you some calamus root right here, Brer Fox. You ought to try it with your chicken tonight!"

Brer Fox leaped off the porch and took off after Brer Rabbit, but that rabbit was halfway to Philly-Me-York before Brer Fox's claws touched the ground. All Brer Fox had for supper that night was an air sandwich.

Brer Rabbit and the Tar Baby

Early one morning, even before Sister Moon had put on her negligee, Brer Fox was up and moving around. He had a glint in his eye, so you know he was up to no good.

He mixed up a big batch of tar and made it into the shape of a baby. By the time he finished, Brer Sun was yawning himself awake and peeping one eye over the topside of the earth.

Brer Fox took his Tar Baby down to the road, the very road Brer Rabbit walked along every morning. He sat the Tar Baby in the road, put a hat on it, and then hid in a ditch.

He had scarcely gotten comfortable (as comfortable as one can get in a ditch), before Brer Rabbit came strutting along like he owned the world and was collecting rent from everybody in it.

Seeing the Tar Baby, Brer Rabbit tipped his hat. "Good morning! Nice day, ain't it? Of course, any day I wake up and find I'm still alive is a nice day far as I'm concerned." He laughed at his joke, which he thought was pretty good. (Ain't too bad if I say so myself.)

Tar Baby don't say a word. Brer Fox stuck his head up out of the ditch, grinning.

"You deaf?" Brer Rabbit asked the Tar Baby. "If you are, I can talk louder." He yelled, *"How you this morning? Nice day, ain't it?"*

Tar Baby still don't say nothing.

Brer Rabbit was getting kinna annoyed. "I don't know what's wrong with this young generation. Didn't your parents teach you no manners?"

Tar Baby don't say nothing.

"Well, I reckon I'll teach you some!" He hauls off and hits the Tar Baby. BIP! And his fist was stuck to the side of the Tar Baby's face.

"You let me go!" Brer Rabbit yelled. "Let me go or I'll really pop you one." He twisted and turned, but he couldn't get loose. "All right! I warned you!" And he smacked the

Tar Baby on the other side of its head. BIP! His other fist was stuck.

Brer Rabbit was sho' nuf' mad now. "You turn me loose or I'll make you wish you'd never been born." THUNK! He kicked the Tar Baby and his foot was caught. He was cussing and carrying on something terrible and kicked the Tar Baby with the other foot and THUNK! That foot was caught. "You let me go or I'll butt you with my head." He butted the Tar Baby under the chin and THUNK! His head was stuck.

Brer Fox sauntered out of the ditch just as cool as the sweat on the side of a glass of ice tea. He looked at Brer Rabbit stuck to the Tar Baby and laughed until he was almost sick.

"Well, I got you now," Brer Fox said when he was able to catch his breath. "You floppy-eared, pom-pom-tailed good-for-nothing! I guess you know who's having rabbit for dinner this night!"

Brer Rabbit would've turned around and looked at him if he could've unstuck his head. Didn't matter. He heard the drool in Brer Fox's voice and knew he was in a world of trouble.

"You ain't gon' be going around through the community raising commotion anymore, Brer Rabbit. And it's your own fault too. Didn't nobody tell you to be so friendly with the Tar Baby. You stuck yourself on that Tar Baby without so much as an invitation. There you are and there you'll be until I get my fire started and my barbecue sauce ready."

Brer Rabbit always got enough lip for anybody and everybody. He even told God once what He'd done wrong on the third day of Creation. This time, though, Brer Rabbit talked mighty humble. "Well, Brer Fox. No doubt about it. You got me and no point my saying that I would improve my ways if you spared me."

"No point at all," Brer Fox agreed as he started gathering kindling for the fire.

"I guess I'm going to be barbecue this day." Brer Rabbit sighed. "But getting barbecued is a whole lot better than getting thrown in the briar patch." He sighed again. "No doubt about it. Getting barbecued is almost a blessing compared to being thrown in that briar patch on the other side of the road. If you got to go, go in a barbecue sauce. That's what I always say. How much lemon juice and brown sugar you put in yours?"

When Brer Fox heard this, he had to do some more thinking, because he wanted the worst death possible for that rabbit. "Now that I thinks on it, it's too hot to be standing over a hot fire. I think I'll hang you."

Brer Rabbit shuddered. "Hanging is a terrible way to die! Just terrible! But I thank you for being so considerate. Hanging is better than being thrown in the briar patch."

Brer Fox thought that over a minute. "Come to think of it, I can't hang you, 'cause I didn't bring my rope. I'll drown you in the creek over yonder."

Brer Rabbit sniffed like he was about to cry. "No, no, Brer Fox. You know I can't stand water, but I guess drowning, awful as it is, is better than the briar patch."

"I got it!" Brer Fox exclaimed. "I don't feel like dragging you all the way down to the creek. I got my knife right here. I'm going to skin you!" He pulled out his knife.

Brer Rabbit's ears shivered. "That's all right, Brer Fox. It'll hurt something awful, but go ahead and skin me. Scratch out my eyeballs! Tear out my ears by the roots! Cut off my legs! Do what'nsoever you want to with me,

Brer Fox, but please, please, please! Don't throw me in that briar patch!"

Brer Fox was convinced now that the worst thing he could do to Brer Rabbit was the very thing Brer Rabbit didn't want him to do. He snatched him off the Tar Baby and wound up his arm like he was trying to throw a fastball past Hank Aaron and chunked that rabbit across the road and smack dab in the middle of the briar patch.

Brer Fox waited. Didn't hear a thing. He waited a little longer. Still no sound. And just about the time he decided he was rid of Brer Rabbit, just about the time a big grin started to spread across his face, he heard a little giggle.

"Tee-hee! Tee-hee!" And the giggles broke into the loudest laughing you've ever heard.

Brer Fox looked up to see Brer Rabbit sitting on top of the hill on the other side of the briar patch.

Brer Rabbit waved. "I was born and raised in the briar patch, Brer Fox! Born and raised in the briar patch!" And he hopped on over the hill and out of sight.

Brer Rabbit Gets Even

About a week later Brer Rabbit decided to visit with Miz Meadows and the girls. Don't come asking me who Miz Meadows and her girls were. I don't know, but then again, ain't no reason I got to know. Miz Meadows and the girls were in the tale when it was handed to me, and they gon' be in it when I hand it to you. And that's the way the rain falls on that one.

Brer Rabbit was sitting on the porch with Miz Meadows and the girls, and Miz Meadows said that Brer Fox was going through the community telling how he'd tricked Brer Rabbit with the Tar Baby. Miz Meadows and the girls thought that was about the funniest thing they'd ever heard and they just laughed and laughed.

Brer Rabbit was as cool as Joshua when he blew on the trumpet 'round the walls of Jericho. Just rocked in the rocking chair as if the girls were admiring his good looks.

When they got done with their giggling, he looked at them and winked his eye real slow. "Ladies, Brer Fox was my daddy's riding horse for thirty years. Might've been thirty-five or forty, but thirty, for sure." He got up, tipped his hat, said, "Good day, ladies," and walked on off up the road like he was the Easter Parade.

Next day Brer Fox came by to see Miz Meadows and the girls. No sooner had he tipped his hat than they told him what Brer Rabbit had said. Brer Fox got so hot it was all he could do to keep from biting through his tongue.

"Ladies, I'm going to make Brer Rabbit eat his words and spit'em out where you can see'em!"

Brer Fox took off down the road, through the woods, down the valley, up the hill, down the hill, round the bend, through the creek, and past the shopping mall, until he came to Brer Rabbit's house. (Wasn't no shopping mall there. I just put that in to see if you was listening.)

Brer Rabbit saw him coming. He ran in the house and shut the door tight as midnight. Brer Fox knocked on the door. BAM! BAM! BAM! No answer. BAM! BAM! BAM! Still no answer. BLAMMITY BLAM BLAM BLAM!

From inside came this weak voice. "Is that you, Brer Fox? If it is, please run and get the doctor. I ate some parsley this morning, and it ain't setting too well on my stomach. Please, Brer Fox. Run and get the doctor."

"I'm sho' sorry to hear that, Brer Rabbit. Miz Meadows asked me to come tell you that she and the girls are having a party today. They said it wouldn't be a party worth a dead leaf if you weren't there. They sent me to come get you."

Brer Rabbit allowed as to how he was too sick, and Brer Fox said he couldn't be too sick to go partying. (God knows, that's the truth! I ain't never been too sick to party. Even when I'm dead, I'll get up out of the grave to party. And when I get sick, the blues are the best doctor God put on earth. The blues can cure athlete's foot, hangnail, and the heartbreak of psoriasis.)

Well, Brer Rabbit and Brer Fox got to arguing back and forth and forth and back about whether he was too sick to come to the party. Finally, Brer Rabbit said, "Well, all right, Brer Fox. I don't want to hurt nobody's feelings by not coming to the party, but I can't walk."

Brer Fox said, "That's all right. I'll carry you in my arms."

"I'm afraid you'll drop me."

"I wouldn't do a thing like that, Brer Rabbit. I'm stronger than bad breath."

"I wouldn't argue with you there, but I'm still afraid. I'll go if you carry me on your back."

"Well, all right," Brer Fox said reluctantly.

"But I can't ride without a saddle."

"I'll get the saddle."

"But I can't get in the saddle without a bridle."

Brer Fox was getting a little tired of this, but he agreed to get a bridle.

"And I can't keep my balance unless you got some

blinders on. How I know you won't try to throw me off?"

That's just what Brer Fox was planning on doing, but he said he'd put the blinders on.

Brer Fox went off to get all the riding gear, and Brer Rabbit combed his hair, greased his mustache, put on his best suit (the purple one with the yellow vest), shined his toenails, and fluffed out his cottontail. He was definitely ready to party!

He went outside and Brer Fox had the saddle, bridle, and blinders on and was down on all fours. Brer Rabbit got on and away they went. They hadn't gone far when Brer Fox felt Brer Rabbit raise his foot.

"What you doing, Brer Rabbit?"

"Shortening up the left stirrup."

Brer Rabbit raised the other foot.

"What you doing now?" Brer Fox wanted to know.

"Shortening up the right stirrup."

What Brer Rabbit was really doing was putting on spurs. When they got close to Miz Meadows's house, Brer Rabbit stuck them spurs into Brer Fox's flanks and Brer Fox took off *buckity-buckity-buckity*!

Miz Meadows and the girls were sitting on the porch when Brer Rabbit come riding by like he was carrying mail on the Pony Express. He galloped up the road until he was almost out of sight, turned Brer Fox around and came back by the house a-whooping and a-hollering like he'd just discovered gold.

He turned Brer Fox around again, slowed him to a trot and rode on up to Miz Meadows's house, where he got off and tied Brer Fox to the hitching post. He sauntered up the steps, tipped his hat to the ladies, lit a cigar, and sat down in the rocking chair.

"Ladies, didn't I tell you that Brer Fox was the riding horse for our family! Of course, he don't keep his gait like he used to, but in a month or so he'll have it back."

Miz Meadows and the gals laughed so hard and so long, they liked to broke out of their underclothes.

Brer Rabbit must've stayed with Miz Meadows and the girls half the day. They had tea and cookies, and Brer Rabbit entertained them with some old-time barrelhouse piano. Finally it was time to go. He kissed the ladies' hands, got on Brer Fox, and with a little nudge of the spurs, rode away.

Soon as they were out of sight, Brer Fox started rarin' and buckin' to get Brer Rabbit off. Every time he rared, Brer Rabbit jabbed him with the spurs, and every time he bucked, Brer Rabbit yanked hard on the bridle. Finally, Brer

Fox rolled over on the ground and that got Brer Rabbit off in a hurry.

Brer Rabbit didn't waste no time getting through the underbrush, and Brer Fox was after him like the wet on water. Brer Rabbit saw a tree with a hole and ran in it just as the shadow of Brer Fox's teeth was going up his back.

The hole was too little for Brer Fox to get into, so he lay down on the ground beside it to do some serious thinking.

He was lying there with his eyes closed (a fox always closes his eyes when he's doing *serious* thinking), when Brer Buzzard came flopping along. He saw Brer Fox lying there like he was dead, and said, "Looks like supper has come to me."

"No, it ain't, fool!" said Brer Fox, opening his eyes. "I ain't dead. I got Brer Rabbit trapped in this tree here, and I ain't letting him get away this time if it takes me six Christmases."

Brer Buzzard and Brer Fox talked over the situation for a while. Finally, Brer Buzzard said he'd watch the tree if Brer Fox wanted to go get his axe to chop the tree down.

Soon as Brer Fox was gone and everything was quiet, Brer Rabbit moved close to the hole and yelled, "Brer Fox! Brer Fox!"

Brer Rabbit acted like he was annoyed when Brer Fox didn't answer. "I know you out there, Brer Fox. Can't fool me. I just wanted to tell you how much I wish Brer Turkey Buzzard was here."

Brer Buzzard's ears got kind of sharp. He put on his best Brer Fox voice and said, "What you want with Brer Buzzard?"

"Oh, nothing, except there's the fattest gray squirrel in

here that I've ever seen. If Brer Buzzard was here, I'd drive the squirrel out the other side of the tree to him."

"Well," said Brer Buzzard, still trying to sound like Brer Fox and not doing too good a job, "you drive him out and I'll catch him for Brer Buzzard."

Brer Rabbit started making all kinds of noises like he was trying to drive the squirrel out and Brer Buzzard ran around to the other side of the tree. Quite naturally, Brer Rabbit ran out of the tree and headed straight for home.

Brer Buzzard was mighty embarrassed when he realized he'd been tricked. Before he could think of what to tell Brer Fox, Brer Fox came marching up with his axe on his shoulder.

"How's Brer Rabbit?" Brer Fox wanted to know.

"Oh, he doing fine, I reckon. He's mighty quiet, but he's in there."

Brer Fox took his axe and—POW!—started in on the tree. He was swinging that axe so hard and so fast, the chips were piling up like snowflakes.

"He's in there!" Brer Buzzard yelled. "He's in there!" The sweat was pouring off Brer Fox like grease coming out of a Christmas goose what's been in the oven all day. Finally, Brer Buzzard couldn't hold it in any longer and he bust out laughing.

"What's so doggone funny?" Brer Fox wanted to know, putting his axe down.

"He's in there, Brer Fox! He's in there!" Brer Buzzard exclaimed, still laughing.

Brer Fox was suspicious now. He stuck his head in the hole and didn't see a thing. "It's dark in there, Brer Buzzard. Your neck is longer than mine. You stick your head in. Maybe you can see where he's at."

Brer Buzzard didn't want to do it, but he didn't have no choice. He walked over real careful like, stuck his head in the hole, and soon as he did, Brer Fox grabbed his neck and pulled him out.

"Let me go, Brer Fox! I ain't done nothing to you. I got to get home to my wife. She be worrying about me."

"She don't have to do that, 'cause you gon' be dead if you don't tell me where that rabbit is."

Brer Buzzard told him what had happened and how sorry he was.

"Well, it don't make no never mind," said Brer Fox. "You'll do just as good. I'm gon' throw you on a fire and burn you up."

"If you do, I'll fly away."

"Well, if that's the case, I better take care of you right here and now."

Brer Fox grabbed Brer Buzzard by the tail to throw him on the ground and break his neck. Soon as he raised his arm, however, Brer Buzzard's tail feathers came out and he flew away.

Po' Brer Fox. If it wasn't for bad luck, he wouldn't have no luck at all.

Brer Rabbit and Sister Cow

While Brer Fox was sitting on the ground with Brer Buzzard's tail feathers in his hand, wondering if God had something against him, Brer Rabbit was eleven miles away. He was tired, sweaty, and out of breath, and when he saw Sister Cow grazing in a field, he thought how nice it would be if she gave him some milk to drink. But he knew she wouldn't. One time his wife had been sick and Brer Rabbit had asked her for some milk and she'd refused him. But that didn't make no never mind. He was going to get him some of her milk.

"How you, Sister Cow?" asked Brer Rabbit, walking up to her.

"Reckon I be getting on all right, Brer Rabbit. How you be?"

"Fair to middling. Fair to middling."

"How's your family?"

" 'Bout the same, I reckon. How's Brer Bull and all your young'uns?"

"They doing fine, just fine."

"Glad to hear it."

Brer Rabbit looked around for a minute and noticed a persimmon tree. "There's some mighty nice persimmons on that tree. I'd love to have some."

"How you gon' get'em?" Sister Cow wanted to know.

"Well, I was wondering if you would butt the tree for me a time or two and shake some down."

Sister Cow allowed as to how she thought she could do that. She took a running start and banged her head into the tree, but no persimmons fell. And there was a good reason too. The persimmons were green and weren't ready to fall, which Brer Rabbit knew. Sister Cow backed up farther and galloped toward the tree like a racehorse and— BAM!—hit that tree so hard that one of her horns got stuck. Brer Rabbit jumped up and did the shimmy, 'cause that was just what he'd been waiting for.

"I'm stuck," called out Sister Cow. "Come give me a hand, Brer Rabbit."

"Don't believe there's much I can do, but I'll run and get Brer Bull." Brer Rabbit ran all right, ran straight home to get his wife and all the children. They come back with buckets and milked Sister Cow dry.

"You have a good night, Sister Cow!" Brer Rabbit called out as him and his family were leaving. "I be back in the morning."

Sister Cow worked hard all through the night trying to get her horn unstuck, and nigh on to daybreak she finally got loose. She grazed around in the field for a while, because she was mighty hungry. Long before the time she thought Brer Rabbit would be coming back, she stuck her horn back in the hole. However, Sister Cow didn't know that Brer Rabbit had been watching all the while.

"Good morning, Sister Cow!" says Brer Rabbit, coming up to her. "How you this morning?"

"Ain't doing too good, Brer Rabbit. Couldn't sleep last night for trying to get out of this hole. Brer Rabbit? You suppose you could grab on to my tail and yank it real hard? I believe if you did that, I might be able to get free."

"Tell you what, Sister Cow. You do the pulling and I'll do the grunting."

Sister Cow had had enough. She turned around and took off after Brer Rabbit. She was a lot faster than Brer Rabbit had given her credit for and it was all he could do to stay a hop in front of her horns. He dived into the first briar patch he saw, and Sister Cow come to a screeching halt.

After a while she saw two big eyes staring out at her. "How you this morning, Brer Big-Eyes?" she says. "You seen Brer Rabbit pass here?"

"I did. He was looking mighty scared too."

Sister Cow went galloping down the road. Brer Rabbit lay there in the briar patch just laughing and laughing. Brer Fox was mad at him; Brer Buzzard was mad at him; and now, Sister Cow was mad at him. And he just laughed and laughed.

———————————

Brer Turtle, Brer Rabbit, and Brer Fox

First thing next morning Brer Rabbit went to see Miz Meadows and the girls. He wasn't far from their house when he came upon Brer Turtle. He knocked on Brer Turtle's roof.

You know, Brer Turtle is a cautious kind of creature and he always carries his house with him. Don't know whether he's afraid of robbers or just what. (The way folks be breaking into houses these days, seems to me Brer Turtle got the right idea.)

Anyway, Brer Rabbit knocked on the roof and asked if anybody was in. Brer Turtle allowed as to how he was. Brer Rabbit wanted to know where he was going.

Brer Turtle thought that was an interesting question, 'cause he hadn't thought about it. Going was so much of a problem that *where* he went wasn't important. Chances were he wasn't gon' get there anyway. As far as he was concerned, he was going to wherever he got to. That being the case, Brer Rabbit said he'd carry him along and they could call on Miz Meadows and the girls. That was all right with Brer Turtle.

Miz Meadows and the girls were glad to have some company and invited them in to set a spell. Brer Turtle was too low to sit on the floor and take part in the conversation, and when they sat him in a chair, he still wasn't high enough. Finally, Miz Meadows put him on the mantelpiece above the fireplace, where he could take part in everything that was going on.

Very quickly the conversation got around to Brer Rabbit riding Brer Fox like a horse the day before.

"I would've ridden him over this morning," said Brer Rabbit, "but I rode him so hard yesterday that he's kinna lame in one leg this morning. I may be forced to sell him."

Brer Turtle spoke up. "Well, Brer Rabbit, please sell him out of the neighborhood. Why, day before yesterday Brer Fox passed me on the road, and do you know what he said?"

Quite naturally nobody did, since they weren't there.

"He looked at me and said, 'Hello, Stinkin' Jim!' "

"He didn't!" exclaimed Miz Meadows. She and the girls were dismayed that Brer Fox would talk like that to a fine gentleman like Brer Turtle.

Now, while all this was going on, Brer Fox was standing in the back door, hearing every word. He sho' heard more than he bargained for, which is always how it is with folks who put their ears in other folks' conversations. The talk about him got so bad that the only way to stop it was to walk in like he'd just got there.

"Good day, everybody!" he said, grinning, and having taken care of all the pleasantries, he made a grab for Brer Rabbit.

Miz Meadows and the girls commenced to hollering and screaming and carrying on. Brer Turtle was scampering around on the mantelpiece and he got so excited that he tripped, fell off, and landed right on Brer Fox's head.

That brought all the commotion to a halt. Brer Fox rubbed the knot on his head, looked around, and Brer Rabbit was nowhere to be seen. Brer Fox looked and looked until finally, he saw some soot falling out of the chimney and into the fireplace.

"Aha!" says he. "I'm gon' light a fire in the fireplace and smoke you out, Brer Rabbit." He started stacking wood in the fireplace.

Brer Rabbit laughed.

"What's so funny?"

"Ain't gon' tell, Brer Fox."

"What you laughing at, I said."

"Well, nothing, except I just found a box of money hid up here behind a loose brick."

Brer Fox wasn't gon' get fooled this time. "That's a lie, and you know it." He commenced to stacking the wood again.

"Don't have to take my word for it," Brer Rabbit said, just as calmly as he could be. "Look up here and see for yourself."

Brer Fox peered up the chimney. Brer Rabbit dropped a brick square on his head. If somebody dropped a brick on your head, that would pretty well take care of things, now wouldn't it?

Brer Wolf Tries to Catch Brer Rabbit

After Brer Rabbit dropped the brick on Brer Fox's head, Brer Fox was laid up in the hospital for a week or so. The day he got out he commenced to scheming again.

He was walking down the road and ran into his cousin, Brer Wolf. They hadn't seen each other since the big family barbecue last Juvember, so they hugged and exchanged news about their kin, and then Brer Fox brought his cousin up to date on all that Brer Rabbit had been doing.

"This has got to stop," says Brer Wolf. "We got to get that rabbit."

"Easier said than done."

"Well, I got a plan, but for it to work, we got to get him inside your house, Brer Fox."

"He wouldn't come in my house if you promised him free lettuce and yogurt for a year."

"Don't you worry about that. I can get him there," says Brer Wolf.

"How?"

"You go home, Brer Fox, get in bed and make like you dead. And don't say nothing until Brer Rabbit puts his hands on you. When he does, grab him, and we got us a good supper!"

Brer Wolf went over to Brer Rabbit's house and knocked on the door. *Bam! Bam! Bam!* Nobody answered. Brer Wolf commenced to banging and kicking on the door like he didn't have no manners, which he didn't. BLAMMITY BLAM BLAM BLAM BLAMMITY!

Finally a teenichy voice came from inside. "Who's there?"

"A friend."

"All them what say friend ain't friend," Brer Rabbit answered. "Who's there?"

"I got bad news."

Bad news will get folks to listen when good news won't. Brer Rabbit cracked the door and peeked half-a-eyeball out.

"Brer Fox died this morning," Brer Wolf said real mournfullike.

Brer Rabbit raised half-a-eyebrow. "That so?"

"He never recuperated from that lick on the head when you dropped the brick on him. I just thought you'd want to know."

This was bad news that was sho' nuf' good news. But it wasn't news to be accepted on somebody else's say-so. He decided to sneak over to Brer Fox's and verify it.

When he got there, everything was quiet and still. He peeped through the open window, and there, lying on the bed, hands folded across his chest, eyes closed, was Brer Fox.

"Po' Brer Fox," said Brer Rabbit. "He sho' is dead. Leastwise he look dead. Of course, I always heard that when folks was dead and somebody came to see'em, dead folks would raise up a leg and holler 'Wahoo!' "

Brer Fox raised up his leg and hollered, "Wahoo!"

Brer Rabbit didn't waste no time getting away from there.

Brer Rabbit Finally Gets Beaten

You know, it ain't possible to go through life without meeting your match some time or other. Brer Rabbit was no exception.

One day he and Brer Turtle were having a good laugh, remembering the time Brer Turtle conked Brer Fox on the head.

Brer Turtle said, "If Brer Fox had chased me instead of you, I would've been caught just as sure as you're born."

Brer Rabbit chuckled. "Brer Turtle, I could've caught you myself."

Brer Turtle looked incredulous. "You must be joking, Brer Rabbit. You couldn't have caught me if your feet had turned to wheels and your tail to a motor."

"Hold on a minute!" Brer Rabbit couldn't believe his big ears. "You so slow that when you moving you look like you standing still."

"I ain't got time to beat my lips with you over it. I got fifty dollars say I'm the fastest."

"And I got fifty say you been shaving the hair off your legs or something, but I know you done lost your mind."

"Brer Rabbit, I hate to take your money, but if that's what you want, that's what you got."

Brer Rabbit laughed. "I'll leave you so far behind that I can plant greens at the beginning of the race and by the time you cross the finish line, them greens will be ready to pick."

"I hope your feet as fast as your mouth."

They got Brer Buzzard to be the race judge and hold the bet money. It was to be a five-mile race, with posts set a mile apart. Brer Turtle claimed he could race faster going through the woods. Everybody told him he was out of his mind. How could he expect to beat Brer Rabbit, who would be running on the road! Brer Turtle said, "Watch me."

Brer Rabbit went into training. He bought a red jogging suit, a green sweatband, and some yellow Adidas sneakers, and he jogged ten miles every day. Then he'd come home and do a whole mess of push-ups, sit-ups, and skip rope to his records. Some folks wondered if he was training for a race or "Soul Train."

Brer Turtle didn't do a thing. You see, it's a strange thing about the Turtle family. There were six of 'em, including Brer Turtle, and they all looked alike. The only way to tell them apart was to put'em under a magnifying glass, and even then you could make a mistake.

On the day of the race, folks was there from all over. Even the TV networks were there, so the folks on the Moon could see it. Miz Meadows and the girls brought lunch baskets and lots of Dr Pepper to drink. Brer Rabbit showed up in his shades, wearing a gold jogging suit with a tan stripe, and when he took that off, he had on emerald-green racing shorts. Everybody ooohed and aaahed and rushed to get his autograph.

Meanwhile, Brer Turtle and his family had been up with the sun. He had put his wife in the woods at the starting line, and he stationed each of his children near the other posts. Brer Turtle hid himself in the woods at the finish line.

Race time came and Brer Rabbit hollered, "You ready, Brer Turtle?"

Miz Turtle was off a little ways in the woods and, disguising her voice, hollered, "Let's go!"

Brer Turkey Buzzard fired the gun and the race was on. Brer Rabbit took off like a 747 jet. Miz Turtle went home.

Brer Rabbit came to the one-mile post. "Where you at, Brer Turtle?"

Brer Turtle's young'un crawled on the road and said, "Right with you, Brer Rabbit."

Brer Rabbit started running a little faster. He came to the two-mile post. "Where you at, Brer Turtle?"

"Right with you," came the answer.

Brer Rabbit ran a little faster. He passed the three-mile post, the four-mile post, and every time he hollered for Brer Turtle, the answer came back, "Right with you!"

The finish line was in sight now, a quarter mile away.

Brer Rabbit could see Brer Buzzard with the checkered flag, but he didn't see Brer Turtle come out of the woods and hide behind the post marking the finish line.

"Give me the money, Brer Buzzard! Give me the money!" Brer Rabbit started hollering, and Miz Meadows and the girls started cheering like they'd lost their senses.

Brer Rabbit was a hundred yards from the finish line when Brer Turtle came from behind the post and crossed the line. "Soon as I catch my breath, I be pleased to take that fifty dollars, Brer Buzzard."

Brer Buzzard handed over the money, and Brer Turtle went home.

Mr. Jack Sparrow Meets His End

Brer Rabbit was mad after he lost the race to Brer Turtle. The neighbors could hear him cussing and carrying on so bad that they almost called the police. Brer Rabbit had to get even with Brer Turtle. But as hard as he thought, as long as he thought, as wide and high as he thought, he didn't have a thought.

That just made him more mad. He decided finally, "If I can't get even with Brer Turtle, then I'll show Miz Meadows and the girls that I'm still the boss of Brer Fox!"

Unfortunately, Brer Rabbit did his deciding out loud. Mr. Jack Sparrow was sitting in a nearby tree, and he heard every word. The period on Brer Rabbit's sentence was hardly dry before Mr. Jack Sparrow started chirping:

"I'm gon' to tell Brer Fox! I'm gon' to tell Brer Fox! Just as sho' as you born, I'm gon' to tell Brer Fox!" And he flew off.

Brer Rabbit got a little worried. To tell the truth, he was downright scared, and he lit out for home. His eyes were on the ground and his feet were in the air and consequently he didn't see Brer Fox until he'd bumped into him and almost knocked him over.

"What's the matter, Brer Rabbit? You in an awful hurry today."

"Brer Fox! I been looking all over for you! What's this I hear about you going to beat me up, beat my wife up, beat my children up, and tear my house down?" He looked mad enough to chew concrete.

"What are you talking about?" Brer Fox wanted to know.

"You heard me! What did I do to make you want to do all that to me and mine?"

"Brer Rabbit, I don't know who told you that, but it's a lie!" Brer Fox started to get a little heated. "Who been telling lies on me?"

Brer Rabbit hemmed and hawed and pretended like he didn't want to say, but finally: "It was Mr. Jack Sparrow. I couldn't believe my ears, but he swore up, down, and sideways that it was the truth."

Brer Fox didn't say another word. He took off down the road looking for Mr. Jack Sparrow. Brer Rabbit smiled and went on home.

Brer Fox hadn't gone far when he heard somebody call his name. "Brer Fox!"

It was Mr. Jack Sparrow, but Brer Fox kept walking like he hadn't heard.

"Brer Fox! Brer Fox!" Mr. Jack Sparrow called, flying around his head.

Brer Fox make like he still ain't heard. Then he came to a tree stump and sat down like he was tired.

"Brer Fox!" said Mr. Jack Sparrow, lighting on the ground beside him. "I got something to tell you."

"Get on my tail, Mr. Jack Sparrow. You know, I'm deaf in one ear and can't hear out of the other."

Mr. Jack Sparrow hopped on his tail.

"Believe you better get on my back, Mr. Jack Sparrow. I'm deaf in one ear and can't hear out the other."

Mr. Jack Sparrow hopped on his back.

"Naw, that won't do either. Still can't hear. Hop on my head."

Mr. Jack Sparrow hopped on his head.

"Doggone it. Believe you better hop on my tooth. I'm deaf in one ear and can't hear out the other, but I got a little hearing in my eyetooth."

Mr. Jack Sparrow hopped on Brer Fox's tooth, and Brer Fox opened his mouth real wide and—GULP!

Tattletales never do come to a good end.

Brer Rabbit Gets Caught One More Time

When Brer Rabbit wasn't getting in and out of trouble, he was courting. Miz Meadows had a sister, Miz Motts, and she moved down from Philly-Me-York. Brer Rabbit decided to court both of them. Now don't come asking me about Brer Rabbit's family arrangements. How folks arranges their families is their business. Ain't yours and it definitely ain't mine.

Courting back in them days ain't like it is now. Well, wait a minute. Come to think of it, I don't know how it is now, being a married man. But back in my time, you took a girl to a restaurant and spent some money; then you took her to a movie show or something like that and spent some more money. She goes home happy and you go home broke. In Brer Rabbit's time, it was the way it's supposed to be: You went to the girl's house before breakfast and stayed until after dinner.

One morning about breakfast time Brer Rabbit went over to see Miz Motts, but she wasn't home. Somebody else might have spent the whole day waiting, or wore themselves out hunting all over the community for her. Not Brer Rabbit. She wasn't home? That was her tough luck! He went on over to Miz Meadows's house, and who should be there but Miz Motts.

Well, they all had a good time that day laughing and talking and carrying on. Long about nightfall Brer Rabbit said he had to go. The ladies asked him to stay for supper. Brer Rabbit was tempted, but it wasn't safe for him to be out after dark, what with the other animals always scheming against him. So he excused himself and headed for home.

He hadn't gone far when he saw a big basket sitting by the side of the road. He looked up the road and didn't see nobody. He looked down the road and didn't see nobody. He looked before and behind and all around. He didn't see nobody. He listened and he listened some more. He didn't hear nothing. He waited and he waited, but nobody came.

Brer Rabbit tipped over to the basket and peeked inside. It was full of grass. He reached in, got a little, and chewed on it for a while, his eyes closed. "Well, it looks like sparrow grass. It feels like sparrow grass. It tastes like sparrow grass, and it seems to me that that's what it is!"

Having reached that scientific conclusion, he jumped up in the air, clicked his heels together, and dived headfirst into all that sweet sparrow grass, and landed right on top of Brer Wolf, who was hiding underneath.

Brer Rabbit knew he was caught this time, but he laughed. "I knew you were in here, Brer Wolf. I knew you by the smell. I was just trying to scare you."

Brer Wolf grinned and licked his lips real slow. "Glad you knowed me, Brer Rabbit, 'cause I knew you the minute you jumped in. I told Brer Fox yesterday that this was the way to catch you, and catch you I did!"

Brer Rabbit got seriously scared and he started begging Brer Wolf to let him go. Brer Wolf's grin got bigger and Brer Rabbit could see the saliva sliding down his big teeth. Brer Wolf climbed out of the basket holding Brer Rabbit by the neck.

"Where you taking me, Brer Wolf?"

"Down to the creek."

"What you taking me down there for?"

"So I can wash my hands after I skin you."

"Oh, Brer Wolf! Please let me go!"

"You make me laugh."

"You don't understand. That sparrow grass made me sick."

"You don't know about sick, Brer Rabbit, until I get done with you."

"Where I come from, nobody eats sick folk."

"Where I come from, them's the only ones we eat."

They got down to the creek and Brer Rabbit was desperate now. He begged and he pleaded and he pleaded and he begged and Brer Wolf grinned and grinned.

Brer Wolf squeezed Brer Rabbit's neck a little harder while he decided what to do.

Brer Rabbit started crying and boo-hooing. "Ber—ber—Brer Wooly—ooly—oolf, if you gon' kill me and eat me, you got to do it right," he blubbered.

"What you mean?"

"I want you to be polite, Brer Wooly—ooly—oolf!"

"And how am I supposed to do that?"

"I want you to say grace, Brer Wolf, and say it quick, please, because I'm getting weak."

"And how I say grace, Brer Rabbit?"

"You fold your hands under your chin, close your eyes, and say, 'Bless us and put us in the crack where Ole Boy can't find us.' Say it quick, 'cause I'm going fast."

Brer Wolf folded his hands under his chin, shut his eyes, and said, "Bless us and—" He didn't get any further, because the minute he folded his hands, Brer Rabbit jumped up off the ground. He took off from there so fast it took his shadow a week to catch him.

The Death of Brer Wolf

Brer Rabbit had tricked Brer Wolf and he was four times seven times eleven mad.

One day Brer Rabbit left his house to go to town, and Brer Wolf tore it down and took off one of his children.

Brer Rabbit built a straw house and Brer Wolf tore that down. Then he made one out of pine tops. Brer Wolf tore that one down. He made one out of bark, and that didn't last too much longer than it takes to drink a milk shake. Finally, Brer Rabbit hired some carpenters and built him a house with a stone foundation, two-car garage, and a picture window. After that, he had a little peace and quiet and wasn't scared to leave home and visit his neighbors every now and then.

One afternoon he was at home when he heard a lot of racket outside. Before he could get up to see what was going on, Brer Wolf bust through the front door. "Save me! Save me! Some hunters with dogs are after me. Hide me somewhere so the dogs won't get me."

"Jump in that chest over there," Brer Rabbit said, pointing toward the fireplace.

Brer Wolf jumped in. He figured that when night came,

he'd get out and take care of Brer Rabbit once and for all.
He was so busy thinking about what he was going to do,
he didn't hear what Brer Rabbit did. Brer Rabbit locked
the trunk!

Brer Rabbit sat back down in his rocking chair and stuck
a big wad of chewing tobacco in his jaw. This here was
rabbit-chewing tobacco. From what I hear, it's supposed
to be pretty good. So he sat there just rocking, chewing,
and spitting.

"Is the dogs gone yet, Brer Rabbit?" Brer Wolf asked
after a while.

"No. I think I hear one sniffing around the chimney."

Brer Rabbit got up and filled a great big pot with water
and put it on the fire.

Brer Wolf was listening and said, "What you doing, Brer
Rabbit?"

"Just fixing to make you a nice cup of elderberry tea."

Brer Rabbit went to his tool chest, got out a drill, and
started boring holes in the chest.

"What you doing now, Brer Rabbit?"

"Just making some holes so you can get some air."

Brer Rabbit put some more wood on the fire.

"Now what you doing?"

"Building the fire up so you won't get cold."

The water was boiling now. Brer Rabbit took the kettle
off the fire and started pouring it on the chest.

"What's that I hear, Brer Rabbit?"

"Just the wind blowing."

The water started splattering through the holes.

"What's that I feel, Brer Rabbit?"

"Must be fleas biting you."

"They biting mighty hard."

"Turn over," suggested Brer Rabbit.

Brer Wolf turned over and Brer Rabbit kept pouring.

"What's that I feel now, Brer Rabbit?"

"Must be more fleas."

"They eating me up, Brer Rabbit." And them was the last words Brer Wolf said, 'cause that scalding water did what it was supposed to.

Next winter all the neighbors admired the nice wolfskin mittens Brer Rabbit and his family had.

Brer Fox and Brer Rabbit Go Hunting

After Brer Rabbit took care of Brer Wolf, Brer Fox decided it was time him and Brer Rabbit became friends. Every time he saw Brer Rabbit you would've thought he was practicing to meet the Queen of England. In a few weeks Brer Fox and Brer Rabbit could be seen sitting on Brer Rabbit's porch in the evening, smoking their cigars and laughing like they was kin.

One morning Brer Fox stopped by and asked Brer Rabbit to go hunting with him. Brer Rabbit didn't feel like doing a thing that day except sitting on the porch and watching his toenails grow, so Brer Fox went off by himself.

He had good hunting that day and caught some pheasant, wild turkey, squab, and a couple of squirrels. By evening his game bag was so full it was busting at the seams.

Well, long about that time Brer Rabbit stretched and thought he'd go and see how Brer Fox had made out. He heard Brer Fox coming along the road, singing loud. "He must've had good hunting," Brer Rabbit muttered to himself.

He hid in the ditch. A few minutes later Brer Fox went by, singing. When Brer Rabbit saw how full his game bag was, his mouth started to water. He ran through the woods until he was some distance ahead of Brer Fox. Then he lay down in the road like he was dead.

A few minutes later Brer Fox came along and saw the rabbit lying in the road. "This rabbit dead," Brer Fox said. "He's fat too." Brer Fox thought for a minute. "Naw, I got plenty game meat," and he went on his way.

Brer Rabbit jumped up, ran through the woods to get ahead of Brer Fox again, and lay down in the road.

When Brer Fox saw what he thought was another dead rabbit, he couldn't believe his eyes. "Here's another one. And this one is just as plump and fat and juicy as the other one." His mouth and nose started to twitch, and his knees trembled just thinking about how good that rabbit would taste. He put down his game bag. "Well, if the Lord wants to provide me with rabbit, ain't no sense in me turning it down. I'll just run back and get that other rabbit, and then come and get this one."

Brer Fox was hardly out of sight before Brer Rabbit grabbed the game bag and went on home.

Next morning Brer Fox came to visit. Brer Rabbit asked him how he had made out hunting.

Brer Fox started foaming at the mouth. "I caught a handful of common sense, Brer Rabbit."

Brer Rabbit smiled. "If I'd knowed that was what you was hunting for, I'd have loaned you some of mine."

Brer Rabbit Tricks Brer Fox Again

When all the animals saw how well Brer Rabbit and Brer Fox were getting along, they decided to patch up their quarrels.

One hot day Brer Rabbit, Brer Fox, Brer Coon, Brer Bear, and a whole lot of the other animals were clearing new ground so they could plant corn and have some roasting ears when autumn came.

Brer Rabbit got tired about three minutes after he started, but he couldn't say anything if he didn't want the other animals calling him lazy. So he kept carrying off the weeds and brambles the others were pulling out of the ground. After a while he screamed real loud and said a briar was stuck in his hand. He wandered off, picking at his hand. As soon as he was out of sight, he started looking for a shady place where he could take a nap.

He saw a well with a bucket in it. That was the very thing he'd been looking for. He climbed, jumped in, and whoops! The bucket went down, down, down until—SPLASH!—it hit the water.

Now, I know you don't know nothing about no well. You probably think that when God made water, He made the faucet too. Well, God don't know nothing about no faucet, and I don't care too much for them myself. When I was coming up, everybody had their own well. Over the well was a pulley with a rope on it. Tied to each end of the rope was a bucket, and when you pulled one bucket up, the other one went down. Brer Rabbit found out about them kind of wells as he looked up at the other bucket.

He didn't know what he was going to do. He couldn't even move around very much or else he'd tip over and land in the water.

Brer Fox and Brer Rabbit might've made up and become friends, but that didn't mean Brer Fox trusted Brer Rabbit. Brer Fox had seen him sneaking off, so he followed. He watched Brer Rabbit get in the bucket and go to the bottom of the well. That was the most astonishing thing he had ever seen. Brer Rabbit had to be up to something.

"I bet you anything that's where Brer Rabbit hides all his money. Or he's probably discovered a gold mine down there!"

Brer Fox peeked down into the well. "Hey, Brer Rabbit! What you doing down there?"

"Who? Me? Fishing. I thought I'd surprise everybody and catch a mess of fish for dinner."

"Many of'em down there?"

"Is there stars in the sky? I'm glad you come, 'cause there's more fish down here than I can haul up. Why don't you come on down and give me a hand?"

"How do I get down there?"

"Jump in the bucket."

Brer Fox did that and started going down. The bucket Brer Rabbit was in started up. As Brer Rabbit passed Brer Fox, he sang out:

> *Goodbye, Brer Fox, take care of your clothes,*
> *For this is the way the world goes;*
> *Some goes up and some goes down,*
> *You'll get to the bottom all safe and sound.*

Just as Brer Fox hit the water—SPLASH!—Brer Rabbit jumped out at the top. He ran and told the other animals that Brer Fox was muddying up the drinking water.

They ran to the well and hauled Brer Fox out, chastising

him for muddying up some good water. Wasn't nothing
he could say.

Everybody went back to work, and every now and then
Brer Rabbit looked at Brer Fox and laughed. Brer Fox had
to give a little dry grin himself.

Brer Rabbit Eats the Butter

The more time the animals spent with each other, the more
they liked it. They got to liking each other so much that
Brer Rabbit, Brer Fox, and Brer Possum decided to live
together. Don't know what their wives and children thought
about it. They probably didn't mind since Brer Rabbit, Brer
Fox, and Brer Possum was never at home nohow.

Everything was going along fine until the roof sprung a
leak. The first sunny day Brer Rabbit, Brer Fox, and Brer
Possum got out the ladder, the hammers and nails, and
climbed up on the roof. They took their lunch with'em so
they wouldn't have to waste time climbing down to eat at
lunchtime. But they realized that the butter would melt in
the sun, so they went and put it in the well to keep it nice
and cool.

They hadn't been working long before Brer Rabbit began thinking about that butter. His stomach started
growling like a cat getting ready to fight. He was ham-
mering and nailing when all of a sudden he jumped up and
yelled, "Here I am! What you want with me?" Off he went
like somebody was calling him.

Brer Fox and Brer Possum watched him go off through
the woods and wondered what was wrong. Brer Rabbit

hid behind a tree and when he saw them go back to working, he sneaked over to the well, whacked off a pat of butter and ate it. Then he went on back.

"Where you been?" Brer Fox wanted to know.

"Oh, I heard my children calling and I had to go see about them. My wife done took sick."

A half hour passed. The memory of that butter began to work on Brer Rabbit's mind, not to mention his stomach. He raised his head, his ears shot up real straight, and he hollered, "Hold on! I'm coming!" Down the ladder he went.

This time he stayed away a little longer, and when he came back, Brer Fox asked, "How's your wife?"

"Mighty low. Mighty low."

Brer Rabbit didn't work more than fifteen minutes when he was off again. He didn't leave the well this time until the butter was all gone. When he got back to the roof he was feeling mighty good.

"How's your wife?" Brer Possum asked.

"She dead," answered Brer Rabbit, with a sorrowful look.

Brer Possum and Brer Fox felt mighty bad. They decided to stop work, eat lunch, and try to make Brer Rabbit feel better. Brer Fox laid out the food and sent Brer Possum to the well to get the butter.

In a few minutes Brer Possum came back all out of breath. "Hey, y'all! Better come quick! All the butter is gone!"

"Gone where?" Brer Fox wanted to know.

"Just done dried up."

Brer Rabbit grunted. "Dried up in somebody's mouth, I bet."

They went to the well, and sure enough, no butter. Brer Rabbit starts looking at the ground real close, like he's Sherlock Holmes or somebody. "I see tracks. If the two of you go to sleep, I can find out who ate the butter."

Brer Possum and Brer Fox went to sleep. Brer Rabbit took the butter left on his paws and smeared it on Brer Possum's mouth. Then he went back to the roof, ate the lunch, come back and woke Brer Fox.

"There's the butter," he said, pointing to Brer Possum's mouth. "He was the one you sent for the butter, wasn't he? He was the first one down here. Couldn't be nobody else but him."

They woke Brer Possum and Brer Fox accused him of eating up the butter. Naturally, Brer Possum denied everything. But Brer Fox pointed to the evidence around Brer Possum's mouth.

Brer Possum kept pleading his innocence. Finally, he had an idea. "I know how we can catch the one what really did it. Build a fire and everybody try to jump over it. The one that falls in is the one what stole the butter."

They built the fire high and they built the fire wide, and when it was going good, the test began. Brer Rabbit was first, and quite naturally, he leaped over the fire so high he didn't even feel the heat. Next came Brer Fox. He got a good running start and managed to make it over, but it was so close that his tail caught on fire. That's why to this day the underside of a fox's tail is white.

Last to go was Brer Possum. He got a good running start, jumped, and—wham!—landed right in the middle of the fire. That was the end of Brer Possum.

I know it don't seem right, since Brer Possum didn't have a thing to do with the disappearance of the butter. But that's the way of the world. Lots of people suffer for other folks' sins. And I could tell you a thing or two about that if I had a mind to.

———————————

Brer Rabbit Saves His Meat

One day Brer Wolf was going home after fishing all day. What's that you say? You say I told you that Brer Rabbit killed Brer Wolf by pouring hot water on him? Well, now, that's true, ain't it? But you got to understand: Back before "once upon a time," dying was different. Just because you died in one story didn't mean you stayed dead for the rest of the stories. That wouldn't be no fun, would it? Of course not.

Now, like I was saying, Brer Wolf was sauntering home with his string of fish when all of a sudden, Miz Partridge came flying out of the bushes at him. He ducked and dodged, wondering what in the dickens was going on.

It finally occurred to him that Miz Partridge must have her nest nearby. Well, Brer Wolf had a lot of fish, but the thought of some nice young partridge was more than he could resist. He dropped his string of fish right there in the road and went to hunt for the nest.

A few minutes passed and along come Brer Rabbit. He stopped when he saw the string of fish lying in the road. He looked at them. The fish looked at him, and that settled that.

When Brer Wolf came back empty-handed, he didn't see nothing in the road but a big wet spot. He looked up the road. No fish. He looked down the road. No fish nowhere.

He sat down and thought the situation over. There was only one explanation, of course: Brer Rabbit!

He went straight there. Brer Rabbit was sitting on the porch.

"You stole my fish," Brer Wolf said without so much as a howdy-do.

"What fish?"

"You know what fish!"

Brer Rabbit said Brer Wolf shouldn't be going around accusing people of crimes they hadn't committed, and Brer Wolf said other folks shouldn't be taking what wasn't theirs, and they went back and forth and forth and back like that until Brer Rabbit said, "If you believe I got your fish, then you can go out back and kill the best cow I got."

Brer Rabbit thought that would put an end to the matter. Nobody would offer his best cow if he was lying. But Brer Wolf knew Brer Rabbit pretty well.

He marched right on back to the pasture, took a close look at all the cows, and being a gentleman of good judgment and discriminating taste, killed the best cow of the lot.

Brer Rabbit couldn't believe his eyes. What was the world coming to when somebody wouldn't believe one of his lies? But that didn't mean Brer Rabbit was whupped.

"Brer Wolf! Brer Wolf! The police is coming! The police is coming! You better run and hide."

Brer Wolf dropped the cow and took off through the underbrush. He was always up to so much no good that it didn't surprise him that the police might be after him.

Brer Wolf wasn't hid good before Brer Rabbit was skinning the cow, cutting it up into pieces and salting it. He called his children and they ran and hid the meat in the smokehouse. When he was finished, Brer Rabbit took the cow's tail and stuck it in the ground.

"Brer Wolf! Hey, Brer Wolf! Come quick! Your cow is going into the ground!"

Brer Wolf came cautiously out of the underbrush and saw Brer Rabbit holding onto the cow's tail like he was

trying to keep it from going into the ground. Brer Wolf grabbed hold. They pulled and—POP!—the tail came out of the ground!

Brer Rabbit shook his head sadly. "We pulled the tail out of the cow and the cow done gone now."

Brer Wolf didn't want to hear nothing like that. He got him a shovel and started digging. Brer Rabbit chuckled and went and sat on his porch. Brer Wolf was shoveling the dirt out so fast you'd a thought he'd turned into a steam shovel. Brer Rabbit just chuckled, and every now and then he sang under his breath:

"He diggy, diggy, diggy, but no meat there. He diggy, diggy, diggy, but no meat there."

Brer Rabbit's Children

Even if Brer Rabbit and Brer Fox had become friends, it didn't mean that Brer Fox had stopped being a fox. When he dropped by to see Brer Rabbit one afternoon and saw the little rabbits all by themselves, well, he couldn't help it that he was a fox. They looked so fat and tender and juicy, he wanted to gobble'em up right then and there, but didn't know how he could without having a good excuse. He still remembered how Brer Rabbit had poured scalding water over his cousin, Brer Wolf.

The little rabbits were huddled in a corner as scared as they could be. Brer Fox sat down in a rocking chair and started rocking back and forth. He saw a stalk of sugar-cane standing by the door. "Break me off a piece of that cane!"

Ain't too many things in this world tougher than sugar-cane. Brer Fox knew they couldn't break it, and when they failed, he'd have an excuse to eat'em.

The little rabbits sweated and they wrestled and they strained and they puffed, but nothing doing.

"You rabbits hurry up! If you don't break me off some of that cane, I'll eat you!"

The little rabbits tried even harder, but they couldn't break it. Then they heard a little bird singing on top of the house:

> *Take your teeth and gnaw it.*
> *Take your teeth and gnaw it,*
> *Saw it and yoke it,*
> *And then you can break it.*

The little rabbits started into gnawing and biting, and

quicker than butter can melt on a hot stove, they had a piece of cane broken off.

Brer Fox wasn't too happy about that. He got up and commenced pacing the floor. He saw a sifter hanging from the wall. "Here! Take this sifter and run down to the creek and get me some fresh water."

The little rabbits ran down there and tried to dip water with the sifter. Naturally the water just kept running out. They didn't know what to do and sat down and cried.

Then, from up in a tree, the little bird started singing:

> *Sifter holds water same as a tray,*
> *If you fill it with moss and daub it with clay;*
> *The Fox gets madder the longer you stay—*
> *Fill it with moss and daub it with clay.*

The little rabbits put moss and clay in the sifter, filled it with water and carried the water to Brer Fox. He was fighting mad now. He pointed to a big log that was setting beside the fireplace. "Put that log on the fire!" he ordered.

The little rabbits tried to lift it. It wouldn't budge. They tried to turn it on end. It wouldn't budge. They tried to roll it. It wouldn't budge. Then they heard the little bird sing:

> *Spit in your hands and tug it and toll it,*
> *Get behind it and push it and pole it;*
> *Spit in your hands and rare back and roll it.*

They set to work and just about time they got the log on the fire, Brer Rabbit and his wife came walking in. Brer

Fox grinned real sheepish like. "Well, Brer Rabbit. Thought you wasn't going to get back before I left."

Brer Rabbit only needed to glance at his children to see that something was wrong, but he pretended like he didn't notice a thing. "Why don't you stay and have supper, Brer Fox? Since Brer Wolf stopped coming to see me, I ain't had much company. Gets mighty lonesome sometime."

Brer Fox allowed as to how Miz Fox was expecting him home for supper, and he tipped on away.

———————————

The Death of Brer Fox

One winter the weather got so cold the animals started wondering if the Lord had forgot to send spring. Most of them were all right, since they'd worked hard during the summer, made a good crop, and got all their wood chopped and stacked. All of them, that is, except Brer Rabbit. He hadn't made a crop that year, since he'd been eating out of everybody else's garden, and he hadn't chopped firewood either, figuring that the winter wouldn't be cold.

Brer Rabbit went over to Brer Fox's house one day and he was troubled in his mind. His wife was sick, his children were cold and hungry, and what little fire there was in the fireplace had gone out in the night.

Brer Fox felt bad, and gave him some fire. Brer Rabbit smelled beef cooking and his stomach almost popped out of his belly, it wanted some of that beef so bad. But Brer Rabbit didn't like to beg, so he took the fire and left. He didn't get far before the fire went out. He went back to Brer Fox's house to get some more.

This time the beef smelled even better. "Brer Fox, where you get so much nice beef?"

Brer Fox answered, "Why don't you come over tomorrow? I'll show you where you can get all the beef you want."

Brer Rabbit showed up bright and early the next day.

"There's a man live near Miz Meadows who's got a lot of cattle. He's got one named Bookay. You just go up to her and say *Bookay,* and she'll open her mouth. You jump in and get as much meat as you can carry away."

Brer Rabbit had never heard of such a thing. "Tell you what. Go with me this time and show me how it's done."

They went down to the man's pasture. Brer Fox walked

around among the cattle until he found the one he was looking for. He walked up to her, hollered *Bookay*, and sho' nuf', the cow's mouth swung open like a door. Brer Fox jumped in and Brer Rabbit jumped in after him.

"Now, you can cut almost anything you want, but don't cut near the haslett [heart and liver]."

"I want me a roast," Brer Rabbit hollered back.

"Fine. Just don't cut near the haslett."

"And after I get a roast, going after some London broil and filet mignon and Chateaubriand."

Brer Rabbit was hacking and cutting and sawing and thinking about the hollandaise sauce he was going to make instead of looking where he was cutting and he cut right through the haslett. The cow fell over dead.

Brer Fox said, "Oh, oh. What we gon' do now? When the man come down this evening to look at his cows, we gon' be in a world of trouble."

"You get in the rear of the cow and I'll get in the head," said Brer Rabbit.

That evening the man came and saw his cow was dead. He cut her open to see if he could figure out what killed her. Brer Rabbit crawled out through the cow's mouth and ran up to the man.

"If you want to know who killed your cow, just look in the hind parts and there he is."

The man didn't take time to look. He got a club, beat on the hind part so hard that he killed Brer Fox dead. Brer Rabbit asked the man if he could have Brer Fox's head. The man cut it off and gave it to him.

Brer Rabbit wrapped the head up in old newspaper and took it over to Brer Fox's house. "Miz Fox, I got some nice beef here that your old man sent for supper. But he said not to look at it until you was ready to eat."

Miz Fox took what Brer Rabbit gave her, put it in the pot and set it cooking for supper. Tobe, Brer Fox's oldest boy, was hungry and got tired of waiting to see what was for supper. He looked in the pot. When he saw what it was, he started screaming and yelling. His momma came running in. When she saw that she was cooking her old man's head, she started screaming.

She called the dogs on Brer Rabbit and he took off running like he'd just heard slavery was coming back. The dogs were so close their tongues were lapping his cottontail. He saw a hollow tree and ducked into it just as the dogs was getting ready to jump him.

Miz Fox and Tobe came along a minute later. She told Tobe to guard the tree while she got the shotgun. After she left, Brer Rabbit asked Tobe if he'd be so kind as to go down to the creek and fetch him some cool water. Tobe, being young and not knowing no better, went to get the water, and quite naturally, Brer Rabbit got out.

When Miz Fox come back and found that Brer Rabbit had gotten away, she was fit to be tied. She told Tobe he wasn't going to live to be no grown fox 'cause she was going to kill him right then and there. Tobe was afraid she meant it, so he went through the woods hunting for Brer Rabbit. Since a fox can outrun a rabbit, it wasn't long before he caught him. He brought Brer Rabbit back to his momma. She took Brer Rabbit by the neck and carried him back to the house.

Brer Rabbit said, "Miz Fox, I know my time is up. I just ask one thing of you. Lay me on the grindstone and grind my nose off so I can't smell when I'm dead."

Miz Fox liked that idea, so she carried him out back to

the grindstone. She looked around and realized she needed some water for the grindstone.

"Tobe can turn the handle," said Brer Rabbit, "while you go and get the water."

Well, soon as Miz Fox left to get the water, Brer Rabbit ran off, and this time Tobe didn't catch him.

Brer Rabbit and Brer Lion

Brer Rabbit was in the woods one afternoon when a great wind came up. It blew on the ground and it blew in the tops of the trees. It blew so hard that Brer Rabbit was afraid a tree might fall on him, and he started running.

He was trucking through the woods when he ran smack into Brer Lion. Now, don't come telling me ain't no lions in the United States. Ain't none here now. But back in yonder times, all the animals lived everywhere. The lions and tigers and elephants and foxes and what 'nall run around with each other like they was family. So that's how come wasn't unusual for Brer Rabbit to run up on Brer Lion like he done that day.

"What's your hurry, Brer Rabbit?"

"Run, Brer Lion! There's a hurricane coming."

Brer Lion got scared. "I'm too heavy to run, Brer Rabbit. What am I going to do?"

"Lay down, Brer Lion. Lay down! Get close to the ground!"

Brer Lion shook his head. "The wind might pick me up and blow me away."

"Hug a tree, Brer Lion! Hug a tree!"

"But what if the wind blows all day and into the night?"

"Let me tie you to the tree, Brer Lion. Let me tie you to the tree."

Brer Lion liked that idea. Brer Rabbit tied him to the tree and sat down next to it. After a while, Brer Lion got tired of hugging the tree.

"Brer Rabbit? I don't hear no hurricane."

Brer Rabbit listened. "Neither do I."

"Brer Rabbit? I don't hear no wind."

Brer Rabbit listened. "Neither do I."

"Brer Rabbit? Ain't a leaf moving in the trees."

Brer Rabbit looked up. "Sho' ain't."

"So untie me."

"I'm afraid to, Brer Lion."

Brer Lion began to roar. He roared so loud and so long, the foundations of the Earth started shaking. Least that's what it seemed like, and the other animals came from all over to see what was going on.

When they got close, Brer Rabbit jumped up and began strutting around the tied-up Brer Lion. When the animals saw what Brer Rabbit had done to Brer Lion, you better believe it was the forty-eleventh of Octorerarry before they messed with him again.

Brer Rabbit Takes Care of Brer Tiger

One year Brer Tiger moved into the community. None of the animals wanted to have a thing to do with him. He was so weird-looking with them black and orange stripes. Not only that, he was big, looked like he didn't have no friends and didn't want none. Everybody kept their distance, everybody except Brer Rabbit.

Brer Tiger was hardly moved into his house good when Brer Rabbit invited him to go for a walk so they could get acquainted.

They were strolling along chatting with one another when they came to a creek. Neither one wanted to wade across and get his feet wet. Brer Rabbit saw a vine hanging from a tree and he swung across to the other side. Brer Tiger thought that looked easy enough, so he grabbed the vine and started to swing across. But he's such a heavy creature that the vine broke and he landed smack dab in the middle of the creek—KERSPLASH!

When he drug himself out and saw Brer Rabbit sitting on the bank laughing, he growled. Brer Rabbit laughed again.

"How come you ain't scared of me like all the other animals?" Brer Tiger wanted to know. "Everybody else run when my shadow hits the ground."

"How come the fleas ain't scared of you?" Brer Rabbit asked. "They littler than me."

Brer Tiger didn't like that kind of sass. "You best be glad I had my breakfast, 'cause if I was hungry you'd be in my stomach now."

Brer Rabbit looked at him. "Brer Tiger, I'm gon' tell you something. If you'd done that, you'd have more sense in you than you got now."

Brer Tiger growled louder. "I'm going to let you off this time, but next time I see you, you mine."

Brer Rabbit laughed. "If you so much as dream about messing with me, I want you to get up the next morning and come apologize."

Brer Rabbit hopped away. Brer Tiger got so mad he grabbed a tree and clawed all the bark off it.

Brer Rabbit was angry too. He shook his fist at the tree stumps and carried on like he was quarreling with his shadow because it was following after him.

He hadn't gone far when he heard a terrible noise. It was Brer Elephant tromping through the woods, eating off the tops of the trees. Brer Rabbit marched up to him.

"Brer Elephant, how would you like to help me run Brer Tiger back where he came from?"

"Well, having him in the community sho' done lowered property values, Brer Rabbit, but I don't know. If I help you, I won't get hurt, will I?"

"What can hurt something as big as you?"

"Brer Tiger got sharp claws and big teeth. He might bite and scratch me."

Brer Rabbit said, "Don't worry about that. Just do what I say and we'll run Brer Tiger away from here."

Early the next morning Brer Rabbit was up and moving about. When he saw Brer Tiger coming, he ran to where he'd told Brer Elephant to wait. Brer Rabbit tied a long vine around one of Brer Elephant's hind legs and tied the other end to a big tree. Then Brer Elephant kneeled down and Brer Rabbit hopped on.

A couple of minutes later Brer Tiger came up and saw Brer Rabbit on Brer Elephant's back. He smiled. He thought Brer Rabbit was caught up there and couldn't get down. Brer Elephant started swinging backward and forward and rocking from side to side.

"Well, Brer Rabbit. I ain't had my breakfast this morning and I sho' am hungry," said Brer Tiger.

"That so?" Brer Rabbit returned. "Well, you just wait till I get through skinning this here Elephant I caught this morning and I'll be down to take care of you."

Brer Rabbit whispered in Brer Elephant's ear: "When I put my nose on your neck, scream loud as you can. Don't be scared. Just scream!"

Brer Elephant screamed so loud he knocked over a couple of trees.

"You wait right there, Brer Tiger. I be done skinning this Elephant in a few minutes."

Brer Rabbit bent over and made like he was nibbling

behind Brer Elephant's ear. Brer Elephant screamed again. A couple of more trees fell.

Brer Tiger started inching backward.

"Where you going, Brer Tiger? I'm almost done. Be down to get you shortly. Just hold on."

Brer Rabbit bent over; Brer Elephant screamed; some more trees fell, and Brer Tiger began putting himself into serious reverse.

"I'm all done now. Elephant blood is all right, but ain't as good as Tiger blood from what I hear."

Brer Rabbit made like he was about to get off the Elephant, but Brer Tiger wasn't around to see if he did or not. He lit off from there and before noontime had moved out of his house and left the community.

Brer Lion Meets the Creature

After Brer Rabbit ran Brer Tiger out of the community, Brer Lion decided he better do something before he got run out. He sent word to the other animals that he was going to eat one member of every family.

Well, there was all kinds of crying and grieving going on in the community, but wasn't nothing the animals could do about it. After a month or so, Brer Lion had eaten his way through every family except Brer Rabbit's. He sent word to Brer Rabbit that it was his turn now.

Miz Rabbit and all the little Rabbits started crying and sniffling and carrying on. Brer Rabbit smoked a cigar like wasn't nothing wrong.

He left the house and went on down the road toward Brer Lion's house. He was almost there when he stopped beside a deep lake. He mussed up his hair and drawed himself in until he was hardly big as a bar of soap that everybody in the family had taken a shower with. Then he looked at himself in the water. He looked like he had one foot in the grave.

He limped and wheezed up to Brer Lion's house. Brer Lion looked at him and shook his head.

"Brer Rabbit, you won't make more than a mouthful. I be hungrier when I get through eating you than I was before."

"I know I ain't fat, Brer Lion, and I probably got a lot of fleas on me. I got a bad cough, and my feets smell, and I got earwax in my navel. But I'm willing. I just want you to know that."

Brer Lion stared hard at him, shaking his head. "I'm gon' have to eat your whole family to get one decent meal if they all look like you."

"Well, Brer Lion, when I was coming over here just now I saw a creature that was as big and fat as you. I said to myself that I wished I was that fat so Brer Lion could have a *good* dinner on me."

"Who was that you saw?" Brer Lion wanted to know.

"Didn't ask his name. I said my how-do's to him and he don't say nothing back. I decided I'd best get on away from him."

"Show me where he is."

"I be glad to, Brer Lion, but I'm afraid of what he might do to you."

"Do to who?" Brer Lion roared. "Show me where he is. We'll see who be doing what to who!"

Brer Rabbit shook his head. "I don't want your death on my conscience."

"TAKE ME TO HIM!"

Brer Rabbit shrugged. "All right. But I be there to back you up. Can't no one animal deal with this creature. He gon' break your legs, Brer Lion!"

Brer Lion was so mad he was trembling. He followed Brer Rabbit to the lake. Brer Rabbit looked around like he was afraid. "He was around here somewhere, and he still around. I can feel it in my bones."

Brer Rabbit creeped forward and looked in the lake. He screamed and jumped back. "He's in there, Brer Lion! Let's get out of here!"

Brer Lion walked up to the lake and peered in. Sure enough, there was a creature looking back at him. Brer Lion hollered at him. Creature in the lake don't say a word. Brer Lion shook his mane; creature shook his. Brer Lion showed his teeth; creature showed his. Brer Lion got so mad that he jumped into the lake head first.

Of course, Brer Lion don't know nothing about swimming and he thrashed around in the lake like he was fighting some creature. He was fighting all right—fighting Ole Boy.

Don't nobody win fights with Ole Boy.

The Talking House

When the animals heard of how Brer Rabbit had gotten rid of Brer Lion, they showed him a new respect. All of them except Brer Wolf. He went over to Brer Rabbit's house one day when everybody was out and sneaked inside.

In the middle of the afternoon Brer Rabbit came home and noticed that everything was mighty still. The door to the house was open a crack. His wife always shut the door tight. He peeped in the windows but didn't see nothing. He listened at the chimney. Didn't hear nothing.

He said to himself, "The pot knows what's going up the chimney. The rafters know who's in the loft. The mattress knows who's under the bed. But I ain't a pot. I ain't the rafters, and I ain't the mattress. But that don't matter. I'm going to find out if anybody's in that house and I ain't going inside to do it either. There're more ways to find out who fell in the pond without falling in yourself."

He went off a ways from the house and hollered, *"Hey, house! How you doing today?"*

House didn't answer.

"HEY, HOUSE! HOW YOU DOING TODAY?"

House still don't answer.

Inside, behind the door, Brer Wolf starts to get a little bit nervous. He ain't never heard of no such goings on as this. He peeped through the crack in the door, but can't see a thing.

"Hey, House! What's the matter? You done forgot your manners?"

Brer Wolf is getting nervous sho' nuf' now.

"Hey, House! You feeling sick today? You ain't never failed to greet me before when I holler."

Brer Wolf decided he better holler back, except he don't know what a house sound like when it hollers. He made his voice as hoarse as he could and hollered, *"Hey, your-self!"*

"You sound like you got a bad cold, House!"

Brer Wolf hollered this time in his own voice. *"Hey, yourself!"*

Brer Rabbit laughed and laughed and then he shouted, *"Brer Wolf! You got to do some practicing if you want to talk like a house!"*

Brer Wolf slunk on away and decided he'd better let Brer Rabbit be for a while.

Brer Rabbit Gets Beaten Again

Brer Rabbit and Brer Buzzard decided to grow a crop together and divide it up at the end of the season.

Come harvest time Brer Rabbit looked at his garden. He had carrots big as fence posts. And cabbage! He had cabbage so big he couldn't fit even one into a wheelbarrow. The lettuce leaves were so wide they looked like shade trees. It was the best crop Brer Rabbit had ever made and he wasn't about to divide nothing with nobody.

He went to see Brer Buzzard. "I don't know how to tell you this, but my garden didn't do well this year. Must've been that dry spell we had a while back. Didn't a thing come up, so I ain't got nothing to divide with you."

"Some years are like that, Brer Rabbit. You just go ahead and take half of what I got, 'cause a deal is a deal."

Brer Rabbit looked around Brer Buzzard's garden and saw peanuts as big as footballs, and ears of corn with such big, juicy kernels they popped open with juice if you looked at'em too hard. Brer Rabbit loaded up and went home, thinking about the good eating he would have all winter.

Brer Buzzard knew Brer Rabbit was lying. All summer he had made daily reconnaissance flights over Brer Rabbit's garden. A few days later Brer Buzzard stopped by to see him. "I just found a gold mine on the other side of the river. But it's too much for me to handle by myself. Give me a hand and I'll divide it with you."

Brer Rabbit didn't need to hear another word. "Lead the way!"

When they got to the river, Brer Rabbit stopped.

"How am I going to get across, Brer Buzzard?"

Brer Buzzard allowed as to how he didn't know.

Brer Rabbit thought for a minute. "How about I get on your back and you fly me over?"

Brer Buzzard was agreeable. They'd been flying for a while when Brer Buzzard lit in the top of a tall pine tree. Brer Rabbit looked down. The pine tree was stuck in the middle of an island and the island was stuck in the middle of the river. Brer Rabbit understood immediately that he had a serious problem.

"I'm sure glad you stopped to rest, Brer Buzzard. Don't see how you do it, but flying makes me dizzy. But, you know, I just remembered something. There's a gold mine near my house. Why don't we go back and dig that one first and then come and dig yours?"

Brer Buzzard thought that was the funniest thing he'd ever heard. He laughed and laughed and laughed until the tree started shaking.

"Wait a minute!" hollered Brer Rabbit. "Hold on! You keep on shaking this tree and I'll fall right in the river."

"That so?" said Brer Buzzard, and started laughing again. "I'll stop laughing if you give me half of your crop what belong to me."

Wasn't a thing Brer Rabbit could do. He divided up his crop and that was that, except he was weak in the knees for a month.

Brer Rabbit Tricks Brer Bear

Brer Rabbit decided gardening was too much hard work. So he went back to his old ways—eating from everybody else's garden. He made a tour through the community to see what everybody was planting and his eye was caught by Brer Fox's peanut patch.

Soon as the peanuts were ready, Brer Rabbit decided to make his acquaintance with them. Every night he ate his fill and started bringing his family, including some second and third cousins of his great-aunt on his daddy's uncle's side of the house.

Brer Fox had a good idea who was eating his peanuts, but he couldn't catch him. He inspected his fence and finally found a small hole on the north side. Brer Fox tied a rope with a loop knot and put it inside the hole. If anybody stepped in it, the rope would grab his leg and hoist'im right up in the air.

That night Brer Rabbit came down to the peanut patch. He climbed through the hole and WHOOSH! Next thing he knew he was hanging in the air upside down.

There wasn't a thing he could do, so he tried to make himself comfortable and catch a little sleep. He'd worry about Brer Fox when Brer Fox showed up the next morning.

Long about daybreak Brer Rabbit woke up, because he heard somebody coming. It was Brer Bear.

"Good morning, Brer Bear," he sang out, merry as Santa Claus.

Brer Bear looked all around.

"Up here!"

Brer Bear looked up and saw Brer Rabbit hanging upside down. "Brer Rabbit. How you do this morning?"

"Just fine, Brer Bear. Couldn't be better."

"Don't look like it to me. What you doing up there?"

"Making a dollar a minute," said Brer Rabbit.

"How?"

"I'm keeping the crows out of Brer Fox's peanut patch."

Brer Bear was overjoyed. He'd been on his way down to the welfare office, 'cause his family had gotten too big for him to support. "Say, Brer Rabbit. Could you let me take over for a while? I need the work and I promise I won't

work too long, but it sure would be a help to me and my family."

Brer Rabbit didn't want to appear too anxious, so he hemmed and hawed before agreeing. Brer Bear let Brer Rabbit down, and Brer Rabbit helped Brer Bear get the rope around his foot and swung him up in the air.

No sooner was Brer Bear swinging in the breeze than Brer Rabbit ran to Brer Fox's house. "Brer Fox! Brer Fox! Come quick! Come quick if you want to see who's been stealing your peanuts."

Brer Fox ran down to the garden and there was Brer Bear.

Before Brer Bear could thank Brer Fox for the chance to make a little money, Brer Fox grabbed a stick and was beating on Brer Bear like he was a drum in a marching band.

Brer Rabbit got away from there as quick as he could.

The End of Brer Bear

A few days later Brer Rabbit happened on Brer Bear, which he hadn't planned on. But he greeted him like they were the best of friends.

"Howdy, Brer Bear. Haven't seen you in a while. How's Miz Brune and Miz Brindle?" Miz Brune was Brer Bear's wife and Miz Brindle was his girlfriend. Don't come asking me how they worked the thing out with each other. From what I hear, folks be doing the same thing now. The animals was doing it long before deodorant, that's all.

Brer Bear said everybody was doing just fine. Brer Rabbit noticed Brer Bear inching close to him.

"Say, Brer Bear," he said quickly. "I got business with you, come to think of it."

"What's that, Brer Rabbit?" Brer Bear said, suspicious-like.

"I was out in the woods back of my house day before yesterday, and I came across one of them old-time honey trees. You know the kind I mean? Them old trees what are hollow from bottom to top and filled with honey?"

Brer Bear smiled. "My granddaddy told me about trees like that, but I ain't never found one."

"Well, why don't you come along with me? Honey ain't

no use to my family. If you don't get it, it's just going to go to waste."

When they got to the woods, Brer Bear said, "I can smell the honey."

Brer Rabbit nodded. "I can hear the bees zooming."

They looked at the tree, wondering how to get the honey.

Finally Brer Rabbit says, "Tell you what. You climb to the top. See that hole up there?" Brer Bear nodded.

"Stick your head in there. I'll get a tree limb and push the honeycomb up to you."

Brer Bear spit on his hands, rubbed 'em together, and shinnied up the tree. Brer Rabbit got a limb and went in the bottom of the tree and started pushing. But he wasn't pushing honeycomb. It was a beehive swarming with bees. He pushed it very gently until the hive was right under Brer Bear's chin.

It's a crying shame the way them bees got on Brer Bear's head. It swelled up so much that Brer Bear couldn't get his head out of the hole. For all anybody know, them bees are stinging him still.

Brer Fox Gets Tricked Again

One time Mr. Man caught Brer Rabbit in his collard green patch. Now don't come asking me what Mr. Man's name was. That ain't in the story. Just Mr. Man. Might have been Slip-Shot Sam. Then again, it could've been One-Eyed Riley. Of course, it might as easily been Freddie Eddie, Freddy Teddy, or Stagolee, 'cepting he never did no work far as I knows. I don't know what Mr. Man's name was, and don't care. Mr. Man is good enough for the story so it's good enough for you.

Like I was saying, Mr. Man caught Brer Rabbit in his collard green patch. Mr. Man had been trying to catch him for a long time and he was overjoyed.

"Got you now! Got you now! I can't get all my greens out of your stomach, but I sure can take some hair off your hide."

He tied Brer Rabbit to a tree alongside the road and went to get a stick. He was going to beat the Devil out of Brer Rabbit and whup some Jesus in. That's the truth!

Brer Rabbit wasn't none too pleased about this turn of events and he was doing some serious scheming when along comes Brer Fox. He saw Brer Rabbit all tied up and stopped to enjoy the sight.

"Somebody finally got you, huh? Fancy that!" He laughed and laughed.

He was laughing so hard it was a moment or two before he realized that Brer Rabbit was laughing right along with him. And laughing harder! "What you laughing at?"

"Just thinking about all the fun I'm going to have when Miz Meadows comes back."

"What're you talking about?"

"Miz Meadows is having a wedding at her house today. She say I got to come, but I don't know as I can. I got to go get the doctor for my children. They sick with the hee-beejitis. Miz Meadows say she don't care. Say if I ain't at the wedding, won't be no fun. She went to town to get the preacher and tied me up to make sure I'd be here when she come back by."

"I ain't heard about no wedding," Brer Fox said, his feelings hurt.

"This is a special wedding and party. She don't invite

just anybody. But I can't go, Brer Fox. I got to go get the doctor. Now I know that if you took my place at the party, Miz Meadows would find that you just as much of a fun man as me and she might stop all her hard feelings about you."

Wasn't nothing Brer Fox wanted more than to be on good terms with Miz Meadows, so he untied Brer Rabbit and let Brer Rabbit tie him to the tree.

"Miz Meadows should be along with the preacher any minute. I sho' nuf' appreciate what you doing for me, Brer Fox." Brer Rabbit hopped into the woods and hid to see what was going to happen.

When Mr. Man came back with a stick big enough to build a house on, he exclaimed, "What! The one what stole my greens has been replaced by the one what's been in my hen house. That's even better." He started in on Brer Fox with the stick. *Blammity-blam-blam-blam.* He beat Brer Fox

until the stick wasn't even good for toothpicks, and went off to get another one.

Brer Rabbit come sauntering out of the woods like he hadn't seen a thing. "That's strange," he said. "Miz Meadows and the preacher should've been here by now. I done been to the doctor's, gone to my house and back, and they still ain't come. That's mighty strange."

"Brer Rabbit!" cried Brer Fox. "Turn me loose from here. Maybe Miz Meadows went the back way." He was trying to pretend like nothing had happened to him.

"Could be," said Brer Rabbit. "Say, Brer Fox? How come your hair is all messed up and your head is all bashed in? Something been bothering you?"

Brer Fox didn't say a word.

Brer Rabbit smiled. "Remember that time you was after my children?" He chuckled. "If there ain't no hard feelings, I reckon I could untie you."

Brer Fox didn't have no choice. He apologized for trying to get Brer Rabbit's children and Brer Rabbit untied him. Just then Mr. Man reappeared with his buggy whip, and Brer Fox and Brer Rabbit didn't waste no time getting away from there.

Brer Rabbit and the Little Girl

If there was one thing in the world Brer Rabbit liked, it was lettuce. He would do anything for lettuce. One day he was going down a road and passed by a field of lettuce, more lettuce than he had seen in all his life! As far as he could see there were rows and rows and rows and rows and rows of lettuce. But between Brer Rabbit and all that lettuce was a wire fence.

Just as he started putting his mind to how he was going to get it, a little girl walked across the road, opened the gate, went in, picked a head of lettuce, and left.

Next morning, bright and early, Brer Rabbit was back. When the little girl came down the road, Brer Rabbit went to meet her.

"Good morning, young lady," he said.

"How you this morning, Brer Rabbit?"

"Just fine. Just fine. Say, you not Mr. Man's little girl, are you?"

"I am," she said proudly.

"Sho' nuf'!" he exclaimed, looking at her admiringly. "He told me about you, but I didn't expect to meet such a pretty young lady."

She blushed. "Why, thank you very much."

"He said he had a daughter who would let me in that field of lettuce over yonder, but I sho' didn't expect nobody as pretty as you."

The little girl just grinned and blushed and giggled. "Well, come on and I'll open the gate for you."

"Obliged," said Brer Rabbit.

He went to a far corner of the field and started eating. And he ate, and he ate, and he ate. The next morning he was back. The little girl let him in again and Brer Rabbit took up where he'd left off. This went on for about a week before Mr. Man noticed he was missing a whole lot of lettuce. He was right angry about it, too, and accused the folks what worked on his place of stealing it. He was about to fire all of them when the little girl said, "Daddy, you must've forgot. You told Brer Rabbit he could have all the lettuce he wanted."

Mr. Man wanted to know what she was talking about, and the little girl told him. Mr. Man nodded. "I see. Well, if Brer Rabbit comes tomorrow, you let him in the field, then come and tell me. There's something I want to talk to him about."

Next morning after the little girl let Brer Rabbit in the field, she went and told her daddy. Mr. Man rushed down to the field with a fishing line and slipped in the gate. Brer Rabbit was eyeball deep in the lettuce, going at it like the statute of limitations on eating was about to expire. Suddenly Mr. Man grabbed him around the neck and Brer Rabbit found himself dangling in the air, staring Mr. Man in the face.

Mr. Man tied Brer Rabbit up tight. "You know what I'm going to do to you?"

"No, but I got a feeling it ain't gon' be to my liking. In fact, I know it ain't."

"It's gon' be to mine. First I'm going to give you a whupping. And for that I got a red cowhide whip. Then I'm going to skin you. Then I'm going to nail your hide to the barn door, and then I just might start all over again from the beginning." Mr. Man told his little girl to watch Brer Rabbit while he went up to the house to get his whip.

No sooner had Mr. Man left than Brer Rabbit began to sing, and he could sing. Women had been known to faint when Brer Rabbit sang. So he started, and this is what he sang:

The Jaybird hunts the sparrow's nest,
The bee-martin sails all around;
The squirrel hollers from the top of the tree,
Mr. Mole, he stay in the ground;
He hide and he stay til the dark drops down—
Mr. Mole, he hide in the ground.

The little girl thought that was the prettiest song she'd ever heard and she laughed and clapped her hands and asked him to sing another one. Brer Rabbit said he couldn't. His throat was hurting from where Mr. Man had been holding him. But the little girl begged and pleaded. Brer Rabbit said, "If you think I can sing, you ought to see me dance!"

"Would you dance for me? Please, Brer Rabbit? Please?"

"How can I dance all tied up like this?"

"I'll untie you," said the little girl.

"You do and I'll show you some dancing."

The little girl untied him, and he danced all right. Danced all the way home. Made up some new steps getting there too!

Brer Rabbit Goes Back to Mr. Man's Garden

Mr. Man's garden was too delicious-looking for Brer Rabbit to leave alone. And anyway, it wasn't right for Mr. Man to have all them pretty vegetables to himself. Obviously, he didn't believe in sharing. Being worried about Mr. Man's soul, Brer Rabbit decided he'd *make* Mr. Man share.

A few mornings later Mr. Man went to town. As he was leaving he hollered to his daughter, "Janey! Don't you let Brer Rabbit get in my green peas. You hear me?"

"Yes, Daddy," she said.

Brer Rabbit was hiding in the bushes, listening. Soon as Mr. Man left, Brer Rabbit walked up to the little girl as bold as day.

"Ain't you Janey?" he asked.

"My daddy call me Janey. What your daddy call you?"

"Well, my daddy dead, but when he was living he called me Billy Malone." He smiled. "I passed your daddy in the road and he said for me to come tell you to give me some sparrow grass."

Janey had been warned against Brer Rabbit, but not Billy Malone, so she opened the gate and let Brer Rabbit into the garden. Brer Rabbit got as much sparrow grass as he could carry and left.

Mr. Man came back and saw that somebody had been in his garden. He asked Janey about it. She told him that Billy Malone said it was all right for him to go in and get some sparrow grass. Mr. Man knew something was up but didn't say anything.

Next morning when he got ready to go, he told Janey to keep an eye out for Brer Rabbit and not let *anybody* get any sparrow grass.

When Mr. Man was out of sight, Brer Rabbit come walking down the road and greeted the little girl, bowing low like a real gentleman. "I saw your daddy just now. He said I couldn't have no sparrow grass today, but it would be all right if I helped myself to the English peas."

The little girl opened the gate and Brer Rabbit made off with enough English peas to feed all of England.

When Mr. Man came back, his pea vines looked like a storm had hit'em, and he was hot! "Who been in my peas?" he asked his daughter.

"Mr. Billy Malone," she said.

"What this Billy Malone look like?"

"He got a split lip, pop eyes, big ears, and a bobtail, Daddy."

Mr. Man didn't have a bit of trouble recognizing that description. He fixed a box trap and set it in the garden among the peanuts. The next morning he told Janey, "Now, whatever you do today, don't let nobody have any sparrow grass, and don't let'em get any more English peas, the few I got left."

Soon as Mr. Man was out of sight, here come Brer Rabbit. He bowed low and said, "Good morning, Miz Janey. I met your daddy down the road there and he said I can't have no more sparrow grass or English peas, but to help myself to the peanuts."

Janey let him in the garden. Brer Rabbit headed straight for the peanut patch, where he tripped the string and the box fell right on top of him. He was caught and he knew it.

Wasn't long before Mr. Man came back. He went to the peanut patch and saw the overturned box. He stooped down, peered through the slats, and saw Brer Rabbit inside, quivering.

Mr. Man whooped. "Yes, sir! I got you this time, you devil! I got you! And when I get through with you, ain' gon' be nothing left. I'm gon' carry your foot in my pocket, put your meat in the pot, and wear your fur on my head."

Words like that always put a chill up and down Brer Rabbit's spine. "Mr. Man, I know I done wrong. And if you let me go, I promise I'll stay away from your garden."

Mr. Man chuckled. "You gon' stay away from my garden if I don't let you go too. I got to go to the house to get my butcher knife."

Mr. Man went to the house, but he forgot to close the garden gate behind him. Brer Fox came down the road, and seeing the open gate, took it as an invitation and walked on in. He heard something hollering and making a lot of racket. He wandered around until he found the noise coming from underneath a box. "What the dickens is that?" he asked.

Brer Rabbit would've known that voice anywhere. "Run, Brer Fox! Run! Get out of here right now if you care about your life!"

"What's wrong, Brer Rabbit?"

"Mr. Man trapped me in here and is making me eat lamb. I'm about to bust wide open I done ate so much lamb. Run, Brer Fox, before he catch you."

Brer Fox wasn't thinking about running. "How's the lamb?"

"It tastes good at first, but enough is enough and too much is plenty. You better get out of here before he catches you."

Brer Fox wasn't running anywhere. "I like lamb, Brer Rabbit." He took the box off Brer Rabbit. "Put the box over me." Brer Rabbit did so gladly and decided not to wait around for the next chapter.

The story don't say what happened to Brer Fox. Brer Rabbit took care of himself. Now it's up to Brer Fox to take care of himself. That's the name of that tune.

Brer Possum Hears the Singing

Brer Rabbit stayed away from Mr. Man's garden for about a month, but he kept having dreams about all those pretty vegetables, and dream-food don't make a meal. No, indeed!

Mr. Man figured that Brer Rabbit would be back and he left the garden gate wide open. He told his daughter, "Janey, I want you to watch careful. If Brer Rabbit or Mr. Billy Malone, or whatever he calls himself, goes in the garden, I want you to run quick and close the gate tight."

"Yes, Daddy."

When Brer Rabbit came and saw the gate open, he thought luck was with him. He ducked in the garden and got down to some serious eating. When he got ready to go, he found the gate closed. He shook it, but it didn't open. He pushed it; it still didn't open. He grunted and pulled on it; the gate didn't budge.

Brer Rabbit hollered, "Hey, Janey! Come open the gate! It hurts my feelings to find the gate shut like this."

Janey came, but she didn't say a word.

"Come on, Janey! Open the gate! It hurts my feelings to see the gate shut like this. If you don't open the gate, I'll tear it off its hinges."

"Daddy told me not to open the gate."

Brer Rabbit opened his mouth wide. "See my long sharp teeth? If you don't open this gate, I'll bite you through and through."

That scared Janey and she opened the gate right quick.

When Mr. Man came back and asked about Brer Rabbit, Janey said, "He was here, Daddy, but I let him out. He said he was going to bite me through and through with his long sharp teeth."

Mr. Man said, "Janey, how is he going to bite you with him on one side of the gate and you the other?"

Janey hadn't thought about that.

Next morning Brer Rabbit went to the garden, found the gate open, went in and proceeded to make friends with Mr. Man's mustard greens. He ate until he was near 'bout green himself. He got ready to go, and lo and behold the gate was shut. He pushed; the gate didn't open. He kicked; gate still didn't open. He butted the gate with his head; nothing doing.

"Hey, Janey!" he hollered. "Come and open this gate! It's bad to mess with a man like me. Very bad! Open the gate."

Janey don't say a word.

"Shame on you," Brer Rabbit told her. "Shame on you doing me like this. You hurting my feelings. Open this gate before I tear it down."

"My daddy told me not to."

Brer Rabbit opened his eyes wide. "See my big eyes? I'll pop one of these eyes at you and kill you dead if you don't open this gate. Open the gate before my eye pops."

Janey hurried right now to get that gate open.

When Mr. Man came back, he asked where Brer Rabbit was. Janey told her daddy he was gone because he was going to pop one of his eyes and kill her.

"Brer Rabbit told a big tale, Janey. He can't do nothing like that."

Next morning Brer Rabbit came, went in the garden, and commenced on the artichokes. He ate artichokes until he was choking. When he got ready to go he figured the gate would be shut, and it was. He pulled it; he shook it; he kicked it; and he cussed it. Gate didn't open.

"Hey, Janey! Come open this gate! It's very bad to treat your own kinfolks like this. It makes me feel so sad when you do me like this."

Janey didn't say a word.

"You ain't supposed to treat kinfolks like this, Janey. Didn't your daddy teach you anything?"

"How you kin to me?" Janey asked.

"Your granddaddy chased my uncle with a dog once. That makes us kin. Now open the gate."

Janey didn't say a word.

"See my long sharp teeth. I'll bite you through and through."

"Not as long as you on that side of the gate and I stay over here."

"See my big eye. I'll pop it at you and shoot you dead!"

"No, you won't. Can't nobody do nothing like that."

Brer Rabbit was hot now. "See my horns!" He made his ears stand up stiff and straight. "I'll run you through."

She ran and opened the gate, and Brer Rabbit got on away from there.

When Mr. Man came back and Janey told him what happened, he said, "Tomorrow when Brer Rabbit comes, you shut the gate and go over to your girlfriend's house and play."

That suited Janey just fine.

Next day Brer Rabbit came and did away with the radishes. When he was ready to go, the gate was shut and he couldn't get it open. He called for Janey, but she didn't come. He tried to find a crack in the fence. No cracks. He looked for a hole. No holes. He tried to jump over. Fence was too high.

Mr. Man came, went in the garden, and grabbed Brer

Rabbit. He tied him in a sack, tied the sack high up on a tree limb, and went off to get his cane.

While he was gone, Brer Possum wandered into the garden. He looked up and saw the bag hanging from the tree limb.

"What's that bag hanging up there for?"

Brer Rabbit said, "Hush, Brer Possum! I'm listening to the singing in the clouds."

"I don't hear no singing, Brer Rabbit."

"Hush, I said! How can I hear if you keep flapping your mouth?"

There was a long pause. "I hear it now!" exclaimed Brer Rabbit. "I wish you could hear the singing in the clouds, Brer Possum."

"So do I."

"Tell you what. I'll let you sit in the bag and listen if you promise not to stay too long."

Brer Possum promised. He climbed the tree, untied the bag, and let it down real slow. Brer Rabbit crawled out and Brer Possum crawled in. Brer Rabbit tied the mouth of the sack real tight and started to pull the rope up to the tree limb.

"I don't hear them singing, Brer Rabbit."

"You will soon enough."

Brer Rabbit tied the sack on the limb.

"I don't hear them singing, Brer Rabbit."

"You'll hear them, Brer Possum. You'll hear them."

Brer Rabbit ran and hid in the bushes.

Just about the time Mr. Man came back, Brer Possum called out, "I don't hear them singing."

Mr. Man said, "I'll make you hear singing!"

Mr. Man took the bag down from the tree, grabbed his cane, and beat on that sack until his arms were tired. Mr.

Man figured Brer Rabbit had to be dead by now. Just as he started to open the sack, Brer Rabbit came out of the bushes and hollered, "I ate your artichokes! I ate your radishes! I ate your peas! I ate your greens, and I'm going to be eating out of your garden until you die!"

_____

Brer Rabbit's Riddle

Mr. Man had almost caught Brer Rabbit, so Brer Rabbit decided it was time to settle down and do some honest work. Maybe he was getting old, or going through a midlife change.

He cleared a piece of ground back of his house and planted the nicest sweet potato patch anybody had ever seen. Brer Fox saw him sweating out there every day and couldn't believe his eyes! Something must've scared Brer Rabbit for him to be putting in a hard day's work. And if Brer Rabbit was living scared, Brer Fox saw his chance to get even for some of the misery he'd suffered.

Brer Fox decided to test Brer Rabbit, and one night he knocked down part of his fence. Next morning Brer Rabbit put it back up. That wasn't the Brer Rabbit that Brer Fox knew. Next night Brer Fox knocked it *all* down. Brer Rabbit patiently put the fence back up and went on to work in his potato patch. Brer Fox made ready to move in for the kill.

Next day he went over to Brer Rabbit's house. "I got a proposition for you. Let's take a walk and talk it over."

"Walk where?" Brer Rabbit wanted to know.

"Right over yonder."

"Where is over yonder?"

"Don't be so suspicious. What I wants to talk to you about is these fine peaches I found. I need your help getting them down."

This was something Brer Rabbit could understand. Before long they came to the peach orchard. Brer Rabbit picked a tree so heavy with peaches it was about to break, and he climbed up. Brer Fox sat at the base of the tree, figuring he would grab Brer Rabbit when he climbed down.

Brer Rabbit knew that, so when Brer Fox told him to throw down the peaches, Brer Rabbit hollered, "Can't! If you miss, the peaches will get squashed on the ground. I'm going to throw them over there in the soft grass."

When Brer Fox went to pick the peaches up, Brer Rabbit hurried out of the tree and ran into the weeds. "Say, Brer Fox! I got a riddle for you."

"What is it?"

"It go like this," and then Brer Rabbit sang:

> *Big bird rob and little bird sing,*
> *The big bee zoom and the little bee sting,*
> *The little man lead and the big horse follows—*
> *Can you tell what's good for a head in a hollow?*

Brer Fox scratched his head and squinched up his face. He scratched his armpit and squinched some more. He scratched his rear and the more he scratched and the more he squinched, the more mixed up he got. Finally, he admitted, "That's a good riddle, Brer Rabbit. What's the answer?"

Brer Rabbit shook his head. "Can't tell you. But I'll give you some help. This is one of them riddles you can't figure out unless you eat some honey. And I know where we can get plenty honey."

Brer Fox followed Brer Rabbit until they came to Brer Bear's backyard, where there were a lot of bee-gums. For all you city folks what ain't been properly educated, a bee-gum is a beehive what's in a gum tree.

Well, Brer Fox didn't have much of a sweet tooth, but he sho' did want to figure out the riddle. He watched while Brer Rabbit walked around among the bee-gums, tapping on them with a stick until he found one that sounded full of honey.

"This is a good one, Brer Fox. Now, put your head in and get some honey."

Brer Rabbit tilted the bee-gum and Brer Fox stuck his

head in. No sooner was it in than Brer Rabbit turned that bee-gum loose and down it came—*ker-swoosh!*—right tight on Brer Fox's neck.

Brer Fox kicked; he squealed; he jumped; he squalled; he danced; he pranced; he begged; he even prayed, but nothing doing. He called out for Brer Rabbit to help him, but shoots! By that time Brer Rabbit was sitting on his front porch smoking a cigar.

After a while Brer Rabbit looked up to see Brer Fox's granddaddy, who folks called Gran'sir' Gray Fox.

"How you today, Gran'sir' Gray Fox?" Brer Rabbit greeted him.

"Not doing too well," Gran'sir' Gray Fox said. "I got the old age in my teeths."

"Sorry to hear that," Brer Rabbit replied. "What brings you over to these parts?"

"You ain't seen that good-for-nothing, triflin' grandson of mine, have you?"

Brer Rabbit chuckled. "I seen him. Me and him been doing riddles. He's off somewhere right now trying to figure out one I gave him. Why don't I tell it to you? If you figure it out, it'll take you right to him."

"All right, Brer Rabbit. Lay it on me."

The big bird rob and the little bird sing,
The big bee zoom and the little bee sting,
The little man lead and the big horse follows—
Can you tell what's good for a head in a hollow?

Gran'sir' Gray Fox put a pinch of snuff in his lip, scratched his head, and coughed a couple of times. He thought and thought and thought and scratched some more, but he couldn't make it out either.

Brer Rabbit laughed and then sang:

Bee-gum mighty big to make a Fox collar,
Can you tell what's good for a head in a hollow?

Gran'sir' Gray Fox put some more snuff in his lip, scratched some more, thought some more, scratched again. Then he smiled, nodded, and headed for Brer Bear's bee-gum trees.

He got there just in time to see Brer Bear catch Brer Fox with the bee-gum on his head. Yes, he got there just in time to see Brer Bear lay into Brer Fox with a hickory stick like Sister Goose battling clothes. Gran'sir' Gray Fox enjoyed the sight too.

––––––––

The Moon in the Pond

Brer Rabbit went to see Brer Turtle one evening. Brer Turtle could tell by his sweet smile that he had some trick in mind, and if anybody was born to be a partner in trickery, Brer Turtle was the man. He was a man among men!

"I got an idea, Brer Turtle."

"Tell me something I don't know."

Brer Rabbit grinned. "I'm going to tell Brer Fox, Brer Wolf, and Brer Bear that I'm having a fishing party down at the pond tomorrow night. I need you to back me up no matter what I say. You understand?"

Brer Turtle said he sho' did. "And if I ain't there tomorrow night, then you know the grasshopper flew away with me," and he laughed.

Brer Rabbit and Brer Turtle shook hands and Brer Rabbit went home and went to bed. Brer Turtle knew that if he was going to be at the pond by tomorrow night he best get started now.

Next day Brer Rabbit sent word to all the animals about the fishing frolic. Brer Fox invited Miz Meadows and Miz Motts as his guests.

That night Brer Bear brought a hook and line. Brer Wolf brought a hook and line too. Brer Fox brought a dip net, and Brer Turtle brought the bait. Miz Meadows and Miz Motts brought themselves dressed up all pretty.

Brer Bear said he was going to fish for mud-cats. Brer Wolf said he was going to fish for horneyheads. Brer Fox wanted to catch some perch for the ladies. Brer Turtle said he'd fish for minnows, and Brer Rabbit looked at Brer Turtle and said he was going to fish for suckers.

They got their fishing poles and what-all ready and Brer

Rabbit went to the edge of the pond to cast first. He drew back his arm to throw his fishing line in the water and suddenly stopped. He stared. The pole dropped from his hand. He leaned forward. He stared. He scratched his head and stared some more. "I don't believe it," he said finally, in a hushed voice.

Miz Meadows thought he might have seen a snake and she hollered out, "Brer Rabbit, what in the name of goodness is the matter?"

Brer Rabbit didn't say nothing, and scratched his head some more. Then he turned around and said, "Ladies and gentlemen, we might as well pack up our gear and go on down to the fish store and buy some fish. Ain't gon' be no fishing at the pond this night."

Brer Turtle said, "That's the truth! That's sho' nuf' the truth."

"Now, ladies, don't be scared. All us brave gentlemen here will take care of y'all. Accidents do happen, but I don't have any idea how this one took place."

"What's the matter?" Miz Meadows asked, exasperated now.

"Why, look for yourselves. The Moon done fell in the water."

Brer Fox looked in and said, "Well, well, well!"

Brer Bear looked in. "Mighty bad, mighty bad!"

Miz Meadows stared at it and squalled out, "Ain't that too much?"

Brer Rabbit shrugged his shoulders. "You can say what you want. But unless we get that Moon out of the water, ain't gon' be no fishing party tonight. You can ask Brer Turtle. He know more about water than anybody here. He'll tell you."

"That's the truth," piped up Brer Turtle.

"How we gon' get the Moon out?" Miz Motts asked Brer Turtle.

"We best leave that to Brer Rabbit."

Brer Rabbit stared up in the sky like he was thinking hard. After a while he said, "Well, if we could borrow Brer Mud Turtle's seine net, we could drag the Moon out."

"Brer Mud Turtle's my first cousin," Brer Turtle said. "I calls him Unk Mud, we so close. He wouldn't mind your borrowing his net."

Brer Rabbit went to borrow the net. While he was gone, Brer Turtle said his grandparents had told him that whoever took the Moon out of the water would find a great pot of money underneath. Brer Fox, Brer Wolf, and Brer Bear got real interested. They said they wouldn't be gentlemen if they let Brer Rabbit do all the work of getting the Moon out of the pond after he done all the work to get the seine net.

When Brer Rabbit got back, they told him they'd take the net and get the Moon out. Brer Turtle winked at Brer Rabbit, and after an appropriate number of protests, Brer Rabbit turned the net over to them.

Brer Fox grabbed hold of one end, Brer Wolf grabbed the other, and Brer Bear came along behind to unsnag the net if it got caught on any logs or debris.

They made one haul—no Moon. They hauled again— no Moon. They went farther out in the pond. The water was getting in their ears. Brer Fox and Brer Wolf and Brer Bear shook their heads to get it out and while they were shaking their heads they got to where the bottom of the pond dropped away, and that's just what they did—dropped off the edge of the shelf right into the deep water. Have mercy! They kicked and sputtered, went under and came up coughing and snorting and went under and came up again.

Finally they dragged themselves out, dripping water like waterfalls.

Brer Rabbit looked at them. "I guess you gentlemen best go home and get into some dry clothes. Next time we'll have better luck. I heard that the Moon will always bite at a hook if you use fools for bait."

Brer Fox, Brer Bear, and Brer Wolf sloshed away, and Brer Rabbit and Brer Turtle went home with Miz Meadows and Miz Motts.

Why Brer Bear Has No Tail

After the trick Brer Rabbit and Brer Turtle played at the pond, they decided to go into business together.

Brer Rabbit went to see Brer Turtle one morning. Miz Turtle said Brer Turtle had gone to visit Brer Mud Turtle. Brer Rabbit went over there and the three of them had a good time sitting around talking and telling jokes.

Way up in the heat of the day they decided to go to the pond and cool off. There was a big slippery rock there that Brer Turtle and Brer Mud Turtle loved to slide down and into the water.

Brer Rabbit sat off to one side and got a kick out of all the fun Brer Turtle and Brer Mud Turtle were having. After a while Brer Bear came along.

"What's going on, folks? I see Brer Rabbit is here, and Brer Turtle and Unk Tommy Mud Turtle is here too."

"Sit down, Brer Bear, and take a load off your feet. We just enjoying the day like there ain't no hard times."

"How come you ain't joining in the fun, Brer Rabbit?" Brer Bear wanted to know.

Brer Rabbit winked at Brer Turtle and Unk Tommy Mud Turtle. "Goodness gracious, Brer Bear! I done had my fun. I was just sitting here letting my clothes dry."

"Maybe Brer Bear might like to join us," suggested Brer Turtle, who was floating on his back in the middle of the pond.

Brer Rabbit laughed real loud. "Who? Brer Bear? You must be joking! His feets are too big. Anyway, his tail is too long for him to be sliding down that rock."

Back in them days Brer Bear had a long pretty tail and it swished angrily. "Who you talking about, Brer Rabbit? You think I'm scared to slide down that rock, don't you?"

Without another word he climbed up on it, squatted, tucked his tail under him, and started down. First he went kinna slow. He was grinning, 'cause this was fun. All of a sudden he got to the slick part of that rock and ZOOM! He was flying sho' nuf' now. Brer Bear swallowed that grin and started screaming. When he hit the water it was like a mountain falling in. So much water went out of the pond, it took until the next summer for it to get filled up again.

Brer Bear walked out of the pond, a sheepish grin on his face. He went back up to where Brer Rabbit was sitting. "Told you I wasn't scared."

Brer Rabbit had his hand behind his back. "You forgot something." He handed Brer Bear his tail.

Brer Bear felt his hind parts and sho' nuf', his tail was gone. It had come off when he hit the slick part of that rock.

"I got some chicken grease at home. It's good for sore places," Brer Rabbit laughed.

Brer Bear was sore all right, but whether he was more sore in his hindparts or his feelings, I just don't know.

Wiley Wolf and Riley Rabbit

There was one period when the animals were getting along so well together, things were almost boring. Brer Rabbit seemed like he'd forgotten how to play tricks. And his best friend was Brer Wolf!

Every Sunday either Brer Rabbit went over to Brer Wolf's or Brer Wolf went to Brer Rabbit's. They were as friendly with each other as the fleas on a dog's back, and they'd sit on the porch and chew tobacco or smoke cigars and talk about all the things they used to do to each other.

While they reminisced, their two oldest boys, Wiley Wolf and Riley Rabbit, played in the yard. Wiley and Riley would jump and run and hide and slide and just have a good time with each other.

"It does my heart good to see our young'uns playing together like they do," said Brer Wolf. "That's how we should've been with each other all these years. I'm just glad our young'uns got better manners than we had."

When it came time for Brer Rabbit to go, Brer Wolf said, "Brer Rabbit, why don't you let Riley Rabbit come over during the week and play with Wiley? I think we ought to do all we can to encourage them to get along."

Brer Rabbit agreed.

Brer Wolf and Wiley walked part of the way home with Brer Rabbit and Riley. When they got to the crossroads, everybody shook hands and Brer Rabbit said Riley would be over to play with Wiley during the week.

Brer Wolf had done a lot of talking about what good friends him and Brer Rabbit had become. But that don't mean his wolf nature wouldn't come on him when he wasn't even looking for it. As he was walking back home with Wiley, he said, "When Riley comes to play with you this week, I think y'all might have fun playing Riding in the Bag."

"What's that, Poppa?"

Brer Wolf was amazed. "You mean I ain't told you about Riding in the Bag? I must not be much of a daddy if I ain't told you about that game. You get in a bag and let Riley pull you around the yard. Then he gets in the bag and you pull him around for a while. That's all there is to it."

When Riley came to visit, him and Wiley played the game and had a good time. But it seemed like Riley didn't have no more sense than to drag Wiley over big rocks and stumps and roots sticking up out of the ground. And when Wiley complained that he was getting hurt, Riley said he wasn't going to do it no more and went right back to doing it.

When Riley went home that night he told Brer Rabbit about the fun game he'd played with Wiley. Brer Rabbit listened and looked thoughtful, but he didn't say anything.

When Wiley told Brer Wolf about how much fun they'd had, Brer Wolf shut his eyes like he was dreaming and began licking his chops.

"There's two parts to the game, Wiley. The second part is called Tying the Bag." He smiled.

Next time Riley came over to play with Wiley, they played Riding in the Bag until they were wore out. Then Wiley suggested they play tying each other up in the bag.

What neither of 'em knowed was that Brer Rabbit was hiding nearby. When he heard Wiley's suggestion, he walked in the yard and called Riley to him.

"It's almost time for you to come home. When Wiley's turn to get tied in the bag comes, tie it as tight as you can. Then run on home. Your momma's got some chores for you."

Brer Rabbit left and Riley and Wiley played tying each other up in the bag for a while. When it was Wiley's turn to get in the bag, Riley tied it as tight as he could.

"I got to run home and do some chores," he hollered to Wiley. "But soon as I'm done, I'll come back and let you out."

If Riley ever went back, I never heard about it.

That evening Brer Wolf came in from working in the field. He saw the bag tied up in the yard and grinned. He was very proud of his son. Wiley didn't feel his father pick up the sack, 'cause he was so wore out from playing that he'd fallen asleep.

Brer Wolf carried the sack inside.

"Ole woman! Is the pot boiling?"

"Sho' is!" she said.

And before you could blink an eye, Brer Wolf dumped the sack in the pot of boiling water.

Brer Rabbit Gets the Money

Brer Rabbit was going along the road when Mr. Man came toward him with a wagon full of money. Now, this wasn't the same Mr. Man whose garden Brer Rabbit had been in. Back in them times people looked alike to the animals, so they called all of them Mr. Man.

Mr. Man was going to town to put his money in the bank. He'd made so much money 'cause he'd had good luck, a long head, a quick eye, and slick fingers.

When Brer Rabbit saw Mr. Man with the wagon full of money he looked around and noticed that he didn't have a wagon full of money. There was something wrong with that. If there wasn't, he'd have the money and Mr. Man wouldn't have any.

As the wagon got close, Brer Rabbit yelled out, "Hold up, Mr. Man! I need a ride."

Mr. Man stopped his wagon. "How come you need a ride, Brer Rabbit? I'm *going* to town and you *coming* from town. We going in opposite directions."

Brer Rabbit grinned. "I'm one of the old-time folks. I don't care which way I'm going as long as I'm riding."

Mr. Man told Brer Rabbit to hop up on the seat. Brer Rabbit allowed as to how he got seasick riding on a wagon seat and he'd just as soon get in back.

The wagon started down a bumpy hill and Mr. Man had to keep his eye on the horses. Brer Rabbit threw some money off and as it hit the ground, he hollered, "*Ow!*"

"What's the matter?" asked Mr. Man.

"Nothing, except you bouncing this wagon so hard it almost knocked my jawbone loose."

They went a little farther and Brer Rabbit flung some more money off, and as it hit the ground he hollered, "*Blam!*"

"What's the matter?"

"Nothing, Mr. Man. I just saw a jaybird fly over and I was pretending like I had a gun."

Brer Rabbit kept on throwing the money off until the wagon was empty. When they got close to town and Mr. Man looked in back, he almost fainted.

"Where's my money? Where's my money? Where's my wagon full of pretty money? Where's my money, Brer Rabbit?"

Brer Rabbit gazed around the wagon like he just noticed that the money was gone. Mr. Man was standing up, tearing his hair and screaming and yelling.

Brer Rabbit shook his head. "Mr. Man. If somebody came along and saw you, they'd think you'd lost your mind." Brer Rabbit looked at the sky. "Sun getting kinna low. It's time for me to be moving on. To tell the truth, Mr. Man, if I stay around here much longer, you be accusing me of taking your money. I appreciate the ride, though."

Brer Rabbit hopped off and headed for home. Of course, on the way he picked up all the money. The thing I can't understand is how come he left Mr. Man with his wagon and horses.

The Cradle Didn't Rock

Mr. Man got sick and tired of Brer Rabbit and his tricks, so he built a trap to take care of him once and for all. Back in them days folks didn't know too much about carpentering, since it had just been invented. They did the best they could, which wasn't none too good if you want to know the truth. So Mr. Man's trap was near about as big as a shed and way too big for Brer Rabbit.

He was making so much racket and doing so much cussing while he was building the trap that it attracted Brer Rabbit's attention. Brer Rabbit couldn't make no sense at all out of what Mr. Man was building, but he kept an eye on him. Don't nobody be building nothing just 'cause it's a sunny day.

When Mr. Man finished, he carried it out in the woods. Brer Rabbit watched Mr. Man put some bait in it and set the trigger. Mr. Man stepped back and smiled admiringly at his trap. Brer Rabbit smiled too.

Now he had a problem. How was he going to get something in the trap so Mr. Man wouldn't be disappointed?

Brer Rabbit set off down the road. Before long he ran into Brer Wolf. They passed the time of day and when Brer Rabbit said he was troubled in his mind, Brer Wolf asked him how come.

"Nothing is going right these days. I just feel plumb wore out."

Brer Wolf's eyes gleamed and his taste buds set to quivering. But he pretended to be sympathetic. "I ain't never heard you talk this way, Brer Rabbit. Why don't you tell me about it? Maybe it make you feel better to talk about it. If there's anything I can do to help you out, I be glad to do it. I'll put my heart into it too." Brer Wolf grinned and his nose started twitching.

Brer Rabbit make like he don't notice. "Well, I'll tell you about it and see what you think. Mr. Man hired me to sit up nights and keep all the creatures and varmints out of his vegetable garden. He say I done such a good job that, in addition to all the greens I can eat from his garden everyday, he'd like to make me a cradle for my little ones. He give it to me this morning, but it's so big and heavy, I had to leave it back yonder there in the woods. I just don't know how I'm ever going to get it home."

Brer Wolf was a little jealous. His ole woman had been on him about getting a cradle for their young'uns. "My wife say cradles is the latest fashion."

"They is, but to tell the truth, I don't care nothing about no cradle. I was only taking this one because Mr. Man was nice enough to make it for me."

"Well, if you don't want it, Brer Rabbit, I be glad to take it off your hands."

Brer Rabbit thought about it for a minute. "Well, the cradle is too big for my young'uns anyway, and just about the right size for yours."

Brer Rabbit took Brer Wolf to where Mr. Man had set the trap.

"There's your cradle, Brer Wolf."

Brer Wolf walked around it. "What's that on the inside?"

"Them's the rockers. It's the latest fashion."

Brer Wolf walked in the trap, sprung the trigger, and there he was.

Brer Rabbit laughed and ducked into the weeds, and not a minute too soon because Mr. Man came up the path to check on his trap. He looked through the slats and clapped his hands. "I got you now! I got you and you ain't getting away this time."

"Got who?" came Brer Wolf's muffled voice from inside. "Who you think you got?"

"I don't think, 'cause I know! Brer Rabbit! That's who!"

"Let me out of here and I'll show you who I am."

Mr. Man laughed and laughed. "You can't change your voice and fool me, Brer Rabbit."

"I ain't Brer Rabbit."

Mr. Man looked through the crack again and saw some short ears. "You may have cut off your ears, but I'd know you anywhere. And I see that you sharpened your teeth, but you can't fool me."

"Ain't nobody trying to fool you, fool! I ain't Brer Rabbit! Look at my nice, bushy tail."

"Uh-huh. You went and tied a tail onto your behind, but you can't fool me, Brer Rabbit."

"I ain't trying to fool you. Look at the hair on my back. That don't look like Brer Rabbit, do it?"

"So you went and rolled in some red sand. You still Brer Rabbit!"

"Look at my black legs. Do they look like Brer Rabbit?"

"Naw, but you put smut on your legs to try and fool me."

Brer Wolf was desperate now. "Look at my green eyes. Do they look like Brer Rabbit's?"

"You can squinch your eyes and make 'em look any way you want, Brer Rabbit. But you can't fool me."

"I AIN'T BRER RABBIT! I AIN'T BRER RABBIT! AND YOU BETTER LET ME OUT OF HERE SO I CAN SKIN THE HIDE OFF BRER RABBIT MY OWNSELF!"

Mr. Man just laughed and laughed and po' Brer Wolf sat down and cried like a little baby.

———————————

Brer Rabbit to the Rescue

Brer Fox was coming from town one evening when he saw Brer Turtle. He thought this was as good a time as any to grab Brer Rabbit's best friend.

He was close to home so he ran, got a sack, and ran back, knowing Brer Turtle wouldn't have covered more than two or three feet of ground.

Brer Fox didn't even say how-do like the animals usually did, but just reached down, grabbed Brer Turtle, and flung him in the sack. Brer Turtle squalled and kicked and screamed. Brer Fox tied a knot in the sack and headed for home.

Brer Rabbit was lurking around Brer Fox's watermelon patch, wondering how he was going to get one, when he heard Brer Fox coming, singing like he'd just discovered happiness. Brer Rabbit jumped into a ditch and hid.

"I wonder what's in that sack Brer Fox got slung over his shoulder?" Brer Rabbit wondered. He wondered and he wondered, and the more he wondered, the more he didn't know. He knew this much: Brer Fox had absolutely no business walking up the road singing and carrying something which nobody but him knew what it was.

Brer Rabbit went up to his house and yelled, "Hey, Brer Fox! Brer Fox! Come quick! There's a whole crowd of folks down in your watermelon patch. They carrying off watermelons and tromping on your vines like it's a holiday or something! I tried to get 'em out, but they ain't gon' pay a little man like me no mind. You better hurry!"

Brer Fox dashed out. Brer Rabbit chuckled and went inside.

He looked around until he saw the sack in the corner. He picked it up and felt it.

"Let me alone!" came a voice from inside. "Turn me loose! You hear me?"

Brer Rabbit dropped the sack and jumped back. Then he laughed. "Only one man in the world can make a fuss like that and that's Brer Turtle."

"Brer Rabbit? That you?"

"It was when I got up this morning."

"Get me out of here. I got dust in my throat and grit in my eye and I can't breathe none too good either. Get me out, Brer Rabbit."

"Tell me one thing, Brer Turtle. I can figure out how you got in the sack, but I can't for the life of me figure how you managed to tie a knot in it after you was inside."

Brer Turtle wasn't in the mood for none of Brer Rabbit's joking. "If you don't get me out of this sack, I'll tell your wife about all the time you spend with Miz Meadows and the girls."

Brer Rabbit untied the sack in a hurry. He carried Brer Turtle out to the woods and looked around for a while.

"What you looking for, Brer Rabbit?"

"There it is!" Brer Rabbit exclaimed.

He took a hornet's nest down from a tree and stuffed the opening with leaves. Then he took the nest to Brer Fox's house and put it in the sack. He tied the sack tightly, then picked it up, flung it at the wall, dropped it on the floor, and swung it over his head a couple of times to get the hornets stirred up good. Then he put the sack back in the corner and ran to the woods where Brer Turtle was hiding.

A few minutes later Brer Fox came up the road, and he was angry! He stormed in the house. Brer Rabbit and Brer Turtle waited. All of a sudden they heard chairs falling, dishes breaking, the table turning over. It sounded like a

bunch of cows was loose in the house.

Brer Fox came tearing through the door—and he hadn't even stopped to open it. The hornets were on him like a second skin.

Yes, that was one day Brer Fox found out what pain and suffering is all about.

———————————

The Noise in the Woods

Brer Rabbit was meandering through the woods one day when he heard Mr. Man chopping down a tree. Brer Rabbit stopped to listen. All of a sudden—KUBBER-LANG-BANG-BLAM!

Brer Rabbit jumped up in the air and took off running. Now, Brer Rabbit might try to claim he wasn't scared, but it's just like lightning and thunder. Folks know that thunder can't hurt'em, but when a loud clap of it come, they get scared and want to run anyhow. Well, that's the way it was with Brer Rabbit that morning.

He ran and he ran and he ran some more, until he was almost out of breath. And about then, Brer Coon came along.

"What's your hurry, Brer Rabbit?"

"Ain't got no time to tarry."

"Is your folks sick?"

"No, thank God. Ain't got no time to tarry!"

"Well, what's the matter?"

"Mighty big racket back there in the woods. Ain't got no time to tarry!"

Brer Coon got kinna skittish, because he was a long ways away from home. He took off running and hadn't gone far when he run smack dab into Brer Fox.

"Brer Coon! Where you going?"

"Ain't got no time to tarry!"

"Is your folks sick?"

"No, thank God. Ain't got no time to tarry!"

"Well, what's the matter, Brer Coon?"

"Mighty queer noise back there in the woods. Ain't got no time to tarry!"

And Brer Fox split the wind. He hadn't gone far when he run smack dab into Brer Wolf.

"Brer Fox! Stop and rest yourself!"

"Ain't got no time to tarry!"

"Is your folks sick?"

"No, thank God. Ain't got no time to tarry!"

"Well, good or bad, Brer Fox. Tell me the news!"

"There's a mighty noise back there in the woods. Ain't got no time to tarry!"

Brer Wolf scratched earth getting away from there. He hadn't gone far before he ran into Brer Bear. Brer Bear asked him what was wrong and Brer Wolf told him about the mighty noise. Brer Bear might have been big but he wasn't slow and he shook the earth getting away. Before long every animal in the community was running like Ole Boy was after them.

They ran and they ran until they came to Brer Turtle's house. Being about out of breath by this time, they stopped to rest. Brer Turtle wanted to know what all the excitement was.

"Mighty noise back there in the woods," Brer Fox said.

"What it sound like?"

None of them knew.

"Who heard the racket?" Brer Turtle asked.

They asked one another and found out that none of them had.

Brer Turtle chuckled. "Excuse me, gentlemen. Believe it's time for me to go eat my breakfast." And he left.

The animals inquired among each other. They weren't surprised to discover that Brer Rabbit was the one what started the news about the noise.

They went over to his house one sunny afternoon and

he was sitting on the porch, getting a tan.

"What you trying to make a fool of me for?" Brer Bear spoke up.

"Fool of who, Brer Bear?"

"Me, Brer Rabbit! That's who."

"This is the first time I've seen you today, Brer Bear."

Brer Coon spoke up. "Well, you seen me today, and you made a fool of me."

"How I fool you?"

"You pretended like there was a big racket in the woods, Brer Rabbit."

"Wasn't no pretend. There was a big racket in the woods."

"What kind?" Brer Coon asked.

Brer Rabbit chuckled. "You ought to ask me that first, Brer Coon. Wasn't nothing but Mr. Man cutting down a tree. If you'd asked me, I would've told you. Sho' would have." And he turned his face up to the sun, closed his eyes, a big smile on his face.

Brer Rabbit Gets the Meat Again

Brer Rabbit was hungry for some meat, Brer Wolf was hungry for some meat, so off they went and killed some-body's cow.

When it was time to divide the meat, Brer Wolf, wary of Brer Rabbit's tricks, said, "I'm the biggest and I should have the most!" He pulled out his butcher knife and started cutting up the cow. Brer Rabbit didn't like that one bit, especially because Brer Wolf was going to take all of it.

Brer Rabbit walked around the cow slowly. He stooped down and sniffed at it. "Brer Wolf? That meat smell all right to you?"

Brer Wolf was steady cutting and carving. He knew what Brer Rabbit was up to. "Smells right fresh. Right fresh."

Brer Rabbit walked around the carcass one more time, squeezing and patting the meat. "It feels flabby to me. How does it feel to you?"

Brer Wolf was steady cutting and carving. "Feels right fresh. Right fresh."

Brer Rabbit got indignant. "I'm trying to be your friend and tell you a thing or two so's you won't die, but you ain't got sense enough to pay me no mind." He stomped off.

A little while later he came back with some fire and a dish of salt.

"What you up to, Brer Rabbit?" Brer Wolf asked suspiciously.

"I ain't taking my share home until I know what's wrong with it."

Brer Rabbit built a fire and carved himself a nice steak. He put it over the fire until it was cooked the way he liked it—medium rare. He nibbled at it; he tasted it; and finally he started chewing. "Maybe I was wrong about this here meat," he said, smacking his lips. He ate the whole thing. "I guess I was wrong, Brer Wolf," he said when he finished, patting his stomach.

Brer Wolf was steady carving and cutting, but kept one eye on Brer Rabbit. Brer Rabbit was sitting on a stump like a judge on a bench.

Suddenly, he threw up his hands and groaned. He swayed backward and forward, groaning. He clutched at his stomach and rocked from side to side. "Oh, Lord! Oh, Lord!"

Brer Wolf stopped cutting. Brer Rabbit's eyes began rolling around in his head. He screamed, fell on the ground, and began thrashing around. "I been poisoned! I been poisoned! Oh, Lordy! Run quick and get the doctor, Brer Wolf! Run quick!"

Brer Wolf got scared and ran for the doctor. But by the time he got back with the doctor, Brer Rabbit was gone. So was the meat. The only thing left was the bill, which the doctor slapped in his hand for wasting his time.

Brer Wolf Gets in More Trouble

Wasn't more than two, three days later when Brer Rabbit met up with Brer Wolf on the road to town. Brer Wolf acted like nothing was wrong.

"Say there, Brer Rabbit! How you be this morning?" Brer Wolf chuckled. "You ought to be 'shamed about the way you tricked me the other day."

Brer Rabbit allowed as to how that was probably true. "How you be, Brer Wolf? How's your folk?"

"Just fine." Then he snarled, "And a whole lot better than you gon' be before this day is over!"

Brer Wolf grabbed for Brer Rabbit. He ducked and off they went through the woods. Brer Wolf was pushing Brer Rabbit for all he was worth. Brer Rabbit began to feel the saliva from Brer Wolf's teeth dropping on his back. He headed for a hollow log he'd picked out for times just like this, a log with holes at both ends.

Brer Wolf saw Brer Rabbit go in, but didn't see him go out. But Brer Rabbit didn't stop to say good-bye either.

Brer Wolf sat down in front of the log to do some profound thinking about what to do to Brer Rabbit, and happened to see Brer Bear clearing new ground.

"Brer Bear! I got Brer Rabbit trapped. Go fetch me some fire!"

When Brer Bear came back with a firebrand, they put it to the log. After a while, it was nothing but ashes. Brer Wolf and Brer Bear smiled, slapped hands, and went home. Had the best sleep they'd had in years that night.

Next day, Brer Wolf went to visit Miz Meadows and the girls. When he got there, Brer Rabbit was sitting on the porch with his arms around them. Brer Wolf almost fainted.

Brer Rabbit wished him how-do and grinned like nothing had ever happened. "Come set a spell, Brer Wolf. Always good to see a good friend like you. Fact is, you a better friend than I ever realized."

"How so?" Brer Wolf wanted to know, still not sure if he was talking to a ghost or if he had lost his mind.

"I was thinking about when you burned me up in that hollow log. When you get the time, I sho' wish you'd do it again."

"Brer Rabbit? One of us is crazy, and it ain't me. What are you talking about?"

Brer Rabbit lowered his voice. "I don't know if I can tell you. I don't want the news to get out."

"I won't tell a soul on the top side of the world."

Brer Rabbit thought for a minute. "All right." He lowered his voice almost to a whisper. "When you get in a hollow log and somebody sets it on fire, honey oozes out all over you. That's what keeps you from getting burned

up. And then you got the job of licking all that honey off."
He chuckled. "That's some job, ain't it? So, please. When
you get time, I got a nice hollow log picked out and it
would be a favor to me if you'd burn me up again."

"I got time right now," said Brer Wolf.

"I knowed you was the kind of man I was looking for."

Off they went. When they got there, Brer Wolf said Brer
Rabbit owed him a favor.

"How so?"

"I burnt you up so you could get the honey. Now it's
your turn to burn me up."

"That ain't fair!" Brer Rabbit exclaimed. "I been looking
forward to getting burned up in this log for days."

They argued the matter back and over until Brer Rabbit
relented. Brer Wolf crawled in the log. (This log wasn't
hollow at both ends.) Brer Rabbit got a pile of leaves and
twigs, stuffed them in the log and put a match to them.
Then he piled up rocks in the opening.

"Getting kinna warm in here, Brer Rabbit, and I don't
see no honey."

"Don't be in a hurry."

The fire got to burning good and the wood was pop-
ping like a gun going off.

"Getting hot now, Brer Rabbit. I still don't see no honey."

"It'll come, Brer Wolf. It'll come."

"I need some air! I'm choking!"

"Fresh air make honey sour. Don't be in such a hurry."

"It's hot in here, Brer Rabbit!"

"That means it's almost time for the honey to come."

"*Ow-Ow!* I'm burning up, Brer Rabbit!"

"Wait for the honey, Brer Wolf!"

"*Ow-ow!* I can't take it no more, Brer Rabbit!"

Brer Rabbit piled on some more leaves and wood. "I'll give you honey. Same kind you wanted to give me."

———————————

Brer Rabbit Tells on Brer Wolf

The animals were divided up into two big groups. There were the ones with claws and long teeth, like Brer Rabbit, Brer Fox, Brer Wolf, and all them. Then there were the animals with horns—folks like Brer Bull, Brer Steer, Sister Cow, Mr. Benjamin Ram, Brer Billy Goat, Brer Rhinossyhoss, and can't leave out Miz Unicorn. There were a lots more, but I can't recollect their names right this minute.

Well, it was late over in the summer one year when the horned animals decided to have a convention and decide what to do about the animals with claws and teeth always chasing them. They went way back out in the woods close to Lost Forty and started their meeting.

Brer Wolf got news of the meeting and sneaked out there to see what was going on. He got a couple of sticks, tied them on his head, and walked up to where a group of horned animals were talking.

"Who you?" Brer Bull demanded to know, eyeing him suspiciously.

"Baaa! I'm little Sook Calf."

Brer Bull wasn't convinced, but he didn't say anything.

Brer Wolf listened to the animals complaining about how he and Brer Rabbit and Brer Fox treated them. He started getting a little nervous. About that time a great big horsefly zoomed by and without thinking Brer Wolf snapped at it.

Somebody laughed loudly.

"Who's making all that racket and showing they ain't got no manners?" Brer Bull bellowed.

Nobody said anything, and after a minute they went back to talking.

Brer Wolf knew that laugh. He ought to, as many times as he had heard it coming at him. Yes, Brer Rabbit had sneaked out to the convention too, and he was hiding in the bushes. When he saw Brer Wolf with them sticks tied on his head and snapping at the horsefly, he couldn't help laughing. Then he sang:

> *O kittle-cattle, kittle-cattle, where are your eyes?*
> *Whoever saw a Sook Calf snapping at flies?*

The horned animals looked around, wondering what that was all about. They went back to talking, but before Brer Wolf could get his ear back in the conversation good, a flea bit him on his neck. Without thinking, he scratched at it with his hind foot.

Brer Rabbit laughed and sang:

> *Scritchum-scratchum, lawsy, my laws!*
> *Look at that Sook Calf scratching with claws!*

Brer Wolf got scared, but none of the horned animals paid him any attention. A few minutes later Brer Rabbit sang out again:

Rinktum-tinktum, ride him on a rail!
That Sook Calf got a long bushy tail!

Brer Wolf was scared sho' nuf' now, especially when he saw Brer Bull looking at him right hard. Brer Rabbit knew this wasn't the time to stop:

One and one never can make six,
Sticks ain't horns, and horns ain't sticks.

Brer Bull and Brer Wolf moved at the same time—Brer Bull at Brer Wolf and Brer Wolf at getting away from there.

Brer Wolf had to keep out of sight for a week or so after that, 'cause Brer Rabbit told everybody that Brer Wolf had been walking in the woods with a chair on his head trying to court Sister Moose.

Brer Rabbit and the Mosquitoes

Brer Wolf had a daughter who was sho' nuf' good-looking. Now, before I go any further I can hear you thinking that Brer Wolf been killed off twice. What that got to do with anything? Am I the tale? Is the tale me? Or is the tale the tale? Well, you can figure that out. If I ain't the tale, and the tale ain't me, it don't make one bit of difference if Brer Wolf was dead or alive. Ain't that so?

Dead or dead, Brer Wolf had a daughter and she was a fine young thing. All the animals was hitting on her! First one was Brer Fox. He was sitting on the porch talking his stuff to her, and everybody know that Brer Fox could talk stuff sho' nuf'. All of a sudden the mosquitoes started coming around. The mosquitoes at Brer Wolf's house was near 'bout big as airplanes and just as loud. Brer Fox started hitting and slapping at them. Brer Wolf came out of the house and told Brer Fox to go. "Any man what can't put up with a few mosquitoes can't court my daughter."

Next was Brer Coon. He hardly got one foot on the porch before he was slapping and biting at the mosquitoes. Brer Wolf showed him how the road run the same both ways.

Next was Brer Mink and he declared war on them mosquitoes. Brer Wolf told him to fight his war somewhere else.

It went on this way until all the animals had eliminated themselves except Brer Rabbit. He sent word that he was coming courting. Brer Wolf's daughter, who had always thought Brer Rabbit was kind of cute, put on her mascara and eyeliner and whatever else it is that the women put on their face. She squeezed herself into a pair of jeans four sizes too small. Have mercy! And she put on a pink halter top! When Brer Rabbit saw her, he thought he'd died and gone to heaven.

When Brer Wolf saw what his daughter was looking like, he said there was no way in this lifetime she was gon' sit there in the porch swing by herself with Brer Rabbit. Not with all he knowed about Brer Rabbit! So he pulled his rocking chair out and sat with them.

They hadn't been there long before Brer Rabbit heard the mosquitoes coming. *Zoom, zoom, zoom.*

"Mighty nice place you got here, Brer Wolf."

Zoom, zoom, zoom.

"Some say it's too low in the swamps," Brer Wolf answered.

Zoom, zoom, zoom.

The mosquitoes were *zooming* so fierce that Brer Rabbit started getting scared, and when Brer Rabbit gets scared, his mind works like a brand-new car motor.

"I was in town today, Brer Wolf, and I saw a spotted horse. Never seen a spotted horse in my life."

Zoom, zoom, zoom.

"Do tell! I ain't never seen one of them myself."

"You're wonderful," said the girl. She figured wouldn't nobody else in the world could've seen a spotted horse. Shows you how far gone she was.

Zoom, zoom, zoom.

"My granddaddy was spotted, Brer Wolf."

"Do tell!"

Zoom, zoom, zoom.

"That's the naked truth I'm telling you. He was spotted all over. He had one spot right here." Brer Rabbit slapped his face and killed one of the mosquitoes.

"I don't want nobody to laugh, but my granddaddy had spots all over. Had that one on the side of his face which I just showed you. Had another one right here on his leg."

Slap!

Another mosquito gone.

"Even had one right here in between his shoulder blades."

Blip!

"And one down here at his hipbone."

Phap!

Brer Rabbit kept on talking about his granddaddy's spots until near 'bout every mosquito in the county was dead. Brer Wolf was so tired of hearing about Brer Rabbit's granddaddy's spots he fell asleep.

At which point, Brer Wolf's daughter dragged Brer Rabbit off to the woods, and the story don't go no further.

How Brer Rabbit Became a Scary Monster

Brer Rabbit was sitting around his house one day with nothing to do, so he decided to pay a call on Brer Bear. Well, not exactly on Brer Bear. On Brer Bear's house!

He sneaked over there and hid in the woods. After a while, Brer Bear, Miz Brune, and Miz Brindle came out and went off down the road like they were going on a picnic. Miz Brune and Miz Brindle had their parasols and Brer Bear was toting a picnic basket. Brer Rabbit waited until they were out of sight and then went in the house.

Brer Rabbit didn't have anything in mind. He was just curious how other folks lived and every now and then went in somebody's house when nobody was home. He peeked in here and poked in there, opened this and rubbed his paws over that. While he was peeking and poking and opening and rubbing, he bumped up against a shelf in the kitchen, and a bucket of honey what Brer Bear kept there tipped over. Before Brer Rabbit knowed it, he was covered with honey, and I mean covered! If you'd seen him, you'd a thought he was a big piece of saltwater taffy. Brer Rabbit couldn't do a thing until the honey dripped off his eyes and he could open'em up to get a good look at the mess he'd gotten himself in this time.

"What am I gon' do?" He was scared to go outside, because he might attract every fly and bee in four counties. But if he stayed in the house, Brer Bear would find him and that would be worst.

So he tipped out of the house and made it to the woods. He commenced to rolling around on the ground, trying to get the honey off. But instead of getting it off, all the dead leaves and twigs and trash what was on the ground stuck to him. He rolled, and the leaves stuck. He rolled the other way, and more leaves stuck. He started jumping up and down and whirling around trying to get the leaves off. He shook and he shivered. He quivered and he quavered. He did a front flip and he did a back flip. He spun around like he was a baton in a majorette's hand. But the leaves and twigs stuck to him like they'd growed there.

"What am I gon' do now?" he wanted to know. Things had just gone from worse to worser. He had to get home and get himself in the bathtub.

He set off through the woods and every step he took, the leaves went *swishy-swushy, splushy-splishy, swishy-swushy, splushy-splishy*. If Sister Ocean had had legs and gone for a walk, I reckon that's what she would've sounded like.

Brer Rabbit was afraid that if anybody saw him, they'd laugh him out of the community, and Miz Meadows and the girls wouldn't allow him to sit on the porch ever again.

He was hurrying across the pasture when he ran into Sister Cow. Sister Cow took one look, raised her tail and took off running like she'd just seen the butcher. Brer Rabbit smiled.

Next person Brer Rabbit run into was a man taking some shoats to market. The man looked at Brer Rabbit. The shoats looked at Brer Rabbit, and I expect the man and them shoats are still running.

Brer Rabbit laughed, but his laugh caught in his throat when he saw Brer Bear, Miz Brune, and Miz Brindle coming back from their picnic. But he squared his shoulders, stood up straight, and walked right at'em. Brer Bear stopped. Miz Brindle, she stopped. Miz Brune, she stopped. Brer Rabbit kept coming. *Swishy-swushy. Splushy-splishy*. Miz Brune throwed down her parasol and ran. *Swishy-swushy. Splushy-splishy*. Miz Brindle throwed down her parasol and ran. Brer Bear stood his ground. Takes more than some swishy-swushy to scare him.

Brer Rabbit jumped up in the air and shook himself real hard. The sound of them leaves scraping on one another sounded like graveyard dirt on dry bones. Brer Rabbit hollered out:

I'm Megog de Roy,
The Devil's baby boy,
My body odor is stronger than you.

That took care of Brer Bear. He dropped the picnic basket, and some farmer lost a whole fence that day 'cause Brer Bear tore it down getting away from there.

Brer Rabbit strutted on down the road and came on Brer Wolf and Brer Fox, who were plotting on how they were going to get him. They was so deep into their plotting that they didn't see him until he was standing right in front of them, excepting they looked up and saw the most awfulest looking creature the world has ever seen.

Brer Wolf wanted to show Brer Fox how big and bad

he was. He looked at the creature and growled, "Who you?"

Brer Rabbit jumped up in the air, shook himself and said:

I'm Megog de Roy,
The Devil's baby boy.
My body odor is stronger than you.

He jumped up in the air again and then charged. Brer Wolf and Brer Fox got away from there so fast they didn't even leave tracks behind.

Brer Rabbit went home, got cleaned up, and then went to see Miz Meadows and the girls. He told them he'd heard that some creature called Megog de Roy had put a scare into Brer Fox. For weeks after, every time Brer Fox showed his face, Miz Meadows and the girls asked him if he wasn't afraid that Megog de Roy might get him.

Brer Fox, Brer Rabbit, and King Deer's Daughter

Miz Meadows and the girls might have been good-looking and pleasant to be around, but there wasn't nobody as pretty as King Deer's daughter. Miz Meadows and the girls couldn't hold a candle to her. She had long black hair and a complexion the color of nutmeg. I won't go into no more details 'cause you too young to be hearing too much.

Both Brer Fox and Brer Rabbit wanted to marry her and they set to courting. One of them was always at her house, and most of the time they were both there. After observing the two of them for a while, King Deer started to favor Brer Fox. He seemed more serious and responsible than Brer Rabbit. Brer Rabbit didn't like that one bit and knew he had to change King Deer's mind.

He was going through King Deer's pasture one day and threw some rocks at two of King Deer's goats and killed them. When he got to King Deer's house, Brer Rabbit asked him, "When is the wedding going to be?"

"What wedding?" King Deer wanted to know.

"The one between your daughter and Brer Fox."

King Deer hadn't put out any news about a wedding. "What you talking about, Brer Rabbit?"

"I thought there was going to be a wedding. I saw Brer Fox down in your pasture throwing rocks at the chickens and killing your goats. I knew he wouldn't be making free with your animals like that if he wasn't going to be a member of your family."

King Deer shook his head. "Brer Rabbit, you don't expect me to believe a tale like that, do you?"

Brer Rabbit shrugged. "Go down to the pasture and see for yourself."

King Deer did, and when he came back he was mad.

Brer Rabbit said, "Now hold on, King Deer. A man shouldn't be too hasty. Don't do nothing to Brer Fox before you sure he the one. Let me talk to him. We're good friends. If he killed your goats, I know I can get him to tell it."

King Deer said, "If you man enough to do something like that, you can marry my daughter."

Brer Rabbit didn't need to hear another word and he set off to find Brer Fox. He didn't go far, because Brer Fox was coming up the road on his way to King Deer's house. He had on his best Sears suit and was looking sharp.

"Where you going?" Brer Rabbit wanted to know.

"Out of my way, Rabbit. I'm going to see my girl."

"That's nice. King Deer told me you were going to marry his daughter."

Brer Fox swelled up so with pride that he popped one of the buttons on his fly.

Brer Rabbit smiled. "King Deer asked me to come around tonight and serenade his daughter as part of the celebration. I told him that you was a music man, too, and how it would be good if I could get you to help with the serenading."

So Brer Rabbit and Brer Fox went off in the woods to practice. Brer Rabbit played the quills, which is what they called pipes back in them times, and Brer Fox played the triangle. Brer Rabbit made up a song for him and Brer Fox to sing. They practiced all through the day, and when night came they went to King Deer's house.

King Deer and his daughter were setting on the porch. Brer Rabbit looked at Brer Fox, counted off the beat, and they started into playing. After they played a tune or two, it was time for the song. Brer Rabbit began singing:

> *Some folks pile up more than they can tote,*
> *And that's what the matter with King Deer's goat.*

Brer Fox sang out:

> *That's so, that's so, and I'm glad that it's so.*

Then Brer Rabbit blew on the quills and Brer Fox played the triangle and Brer Rabbit sang the next verse:

Some kill sheep and some kill shoats,
But Brer Fox kill King Deer's goats.

King Deer didn't need to hear another word. He came off the porch and went upside Brer Fox's head with his walking stick, and Brer Fox took off down the road.

King Deer's daughter invited Brer Rabbit to sit a while with her. Now, some say they got married. Some say they didn't. I don't know, and to tell the truth, don't much care, 'cause that ain't what the story was about. If you worried about it, make up your own story.

———————————

Brer Rabbit Breaks Up the Party

Like I said at the beginning, if there was one thing the animals agreed on, it was partying. If the sun came up on time, they had a party! If the rain was wet, they partied! If the grass was green, they partied!

One day Brer Fox decided to have a party because it was Tuesday. He invited Brer Bear, Brer Wolf, Brer Coon, and some of the other animals, but he didn't invite Brer Rabbit.

The animals got to Brer Fox's and he poured the liquor, turned on the radio, and the animals got to dancing and drinking and telling jokes and just having a good time.

Quite naturally, Brer Rabbit heard about the party and decided to invite himself. He went up to the attic of his house and got an old drum he had and headed to Brer Fox's.

The animals had just started partying good when all of

a sudden they heard this noise like thunder mixed with hail—*Diddybum, diddybum, diddybum-bum-bum-bum—diddybum!*

Brer Coon, who always had one ear out the window, said, "Turn down that radio, y'all!"

Diddybum, diddybum, diddybum-bum-bum—diddybum!

"What's that?" Brer Coon wanted to know.

Diddybum, diddybum, diddybum-bum-bum—diddybum!

Brer Coon reached under his chair for his hat. "Well, gentlemen, I believe it's time I headed for home. I told the ole lady that I wouldn't be gone more than a minute and here it is getting on toward moon-up." He started toward the door, walking slow, like he was cool. By the time he reached the back gate, here come the other animals with Brer Fox in the lead. Them animals kicked up a small dust storm getting into the woods.

Brer Rabbit came on toward the house—*Diddybum, diddybum, diddybum-bum-bum—diddybum!* When he got there, everybody was gone. Brer Rabbit kicked open the door, walked in and hollered, "Brer Fox! Where you at?"

Wasn't no answer and Brer Rabbit laughed. He sat down in Brer Fox's easy chair, spit on the floor, and laughed some more.

He looked around and saw the liquor sitting on the sideboard. He poured himself a drink. Then he poured himself another one. Before long Brer Rabbit was feeling mighty good.

Meanwhile the animals was down there in the woods listening for the *diddy-bum*. They didn't hear it for a long while, and Brer Fox, feeling kind of foolish now, said, "Come on. Let's get back to the party. Brer Coon come scaring us for nothing."

They headed back to the house real slowlike. Fact of the matter is, they creeped back. If somebody had shook a bush, them animals would've jumped out of their skins.

They peeped in the windows and saw Brer Rabbit standing by the sideboard drinking like liquor was about to be outlawed. By now he wasn't none too steady on his legs and Brer Fox saw his chance.

He bust in the door. "I got you now, Brer Rabbit! I got you now!" Him and the other animals surrounded Brer Rabbit.

Brer Rabbit was a long way from being drunk, but he pretended he was drunker than he was. He staggered around the room the way a butterfly go through the air. He looked at Brer Fox kinna cross-eyed, slapped him on the back, and hollered, "How's your mama?" And he giggled.

Brer Fox was ready to get down to business, the business being what they were going to do with Brer Rabbit. Brer Bear was the judge among all the animals, so he put on his glasses and cleared his throat.

"According to the law, the best way to deal with a creature that has been a pest in the community like Brer Rabbit is to drown him." And saying that, he took off his glasses.

Brer Fox, who was the jury foreman, clapped his hands and say he sho' nuf' like the law. So it was agreed to drown Brer Rabbit in the creek.

Brer Rabbit didn't like that idea at all. He started trembling and hollered out in a pitiful voice, "In the name of goodness, please don't fling me in the creek! Y'all know I can't swim. If you gon' throw me in the creek, then have some pity on me and let me have a walking stick so's I can have something to hold onto while I drown."

Brer Fox looked at Brer Bear. Brer Bear put his glasses back on, scratched his head, mumbled to himself, and said, finally, "Well, I don't remember nothing in the law that would be against it." And he took his glasses off.

They gave Brer Rabbit a walking stick, carried him down to the creek and threw him in. Brer Rabbit landed on his feet, and using the stick, walked across. It wasn't no more than knee-deep to begin with.

When Brer Rabbit got to the other side, he hollered back, "I sho' wish you'd stop buying that cheap liquor, Brer Fox!" And with that, he was gone!

Brer Rabbit Outwits Mr. Man

You remember how Brer Rabbit tricked Brer Bear into getting tied in the tree? Well, after that, Brer Bear decided to find a job. He finally got one as the ferryman on the big river. Before long all the animals agreed that Brer Bear had natural talent for the job. He could take the ferry back and forth across the river so smooth you didn't even know you were moving.

Once Mr. Man came down to the ferry with a mare and a colt. Brer Bear let down the plank for the mare and the colt to come aboard. That was where the trouble started.

Mr. Man got in front to lead the mare on. She went halfway and balked. Mr. Man pulled and the mare dug in her hind legs. Mr. Man pushed and the mare dug in her front legs. Mr. Man tried to ride her on board. She dug in both legs and you'd of thought she'd suddenly turned to

stone. The colt thought Mr. Man was trying to do something to its mama, and it started running around like a pig
with hot dishwater on its back.

Mr. Man decided to study on the situation for a while.
He studied. Brer Bear sat down next to him and he studied. Between the two of them they didn't get one idea.

Finally Brer Bear decided to give up thinking. It had never
been one of his virtues anyway. He looked around and saw
Brer Rabbit sitting on a stump, laughing and holding his
sides.

Brer Bear went over to him. "What's so funny?"

"You and Mr. Man," Brer Rabbit said.

"Instead of sitting here laughing at us, why don't you
help us get that mare and colt on the ferry? With three of
us working at it, we could get 'em on."

Brer Rabbit shook his head. "How come I want to do

that? I wouldn't have nothing to laugh at." And Brer Rabbit broke up again.

Brer Bear gave a dry grin and started to walk away.

"Hold up there, Brer Bear!" Brer Rabbit called to him. "I guess I done laughed enough. Getting that mare and that colt on the ferry is easy as going to sleep in a swing."

Brer Bear said, "If you help us get that colt on the ferry, I'll do anything you want me to."

Brer Rabbit shrugged. "All you got to do is pick up the colt and put it on. Its mama will just naturally follow."

Brer Bear went wobbling back to the ferry, picked up the colt and put it on. Just like Brer Rabbit had said, the mare walked on the ferryboat like she'd been born there.

Mr. Man wanted to know how he'd figured that out. Brer Bear told him that Brer Rabbit had done the figuring. "Brer Rabbit is something else!" Brer Bear exclaimed proudly. "He's not only the smartest one of all us animals. He's even smarter than people. Can't nobody fool him and can't nobody outdo him."

Mr. Man didn't like that. "We'll see about that. I be back in a day or two and I bet you a pot of honey against a dish of cream that I can outdo Brer Rabbit."

Brer Bear smiled. "That's a bet!"

A couple of days later Mr. Man came back and he had two mares with him. Them two mares looked exactly alike. They were the same color, same size, and even had the same gait.

After Brer Bear had ferried Mr. Man across, Mr. Man said, "One of these mares is the mama and the other one is the daughter. Now, go get Brer Rabbit and ask him to tell me which is which."

Brer Bear looked at the two mares and he was sorry he

had made the bet. Wasn't no way Brer Rabbit was going to be able to tell which was which. He shook his head.

Mr. Man laughed. "Give me my dish of cream!"

But Brer Bear could smell the pot of honey Mr. Man had in his saddlebags.

"Give me my dish of cream!" Mr. Man repeated.

Brer Bear wasn't going to give up a dish of cream just like that. He went up on the hill and called Brer Rabbit. Brer Rabbit had been staying in the vicinity, waiting for Mr. Man to come back, so he came running.

"I apologize, Brer Rabbit, for getting you into all this. I just hope you won't be too mad at me." He explained the puzzle to Brer Rabbit. Brer Rabbit chuckled.

"Brer Bear, tell you what you do. Get two bunches of grass and put them in front of the mares."

Brer Bear did as Brer Rabbit told him. Brer Rabbit watched as the mares started eating. One mare ate all her grass first and started to eating the other mare's grass. That mare held up her head so the first mare could eat that grass too.

"The one holding up her head is the mama," said Brer Rabbit.

Mr. Man's mouth fell open. "That's right! How did you know?"

"Easy. The youngest one eats the fastest, being young and all. Being the youngest, she's also the hungriest. And the mama stopped eating hers so that the youngest could have that too."

Mr. Man was astonished, but he still wasn't satisfied that a rabbit could be smarter than a person. He gave Brer Bear the pot of honey.

"I bet you another pot of honey that I can fool Brer Rabbit!"

"Bet!" said Brer Bear, licking at the honey pot.

"Y'all wait right here."

Mr. Man went off. In a little while he was back carrying a basket. He held the basket up high so Brer Rabbit couldn't see inside and then hung it in a tree limb.

"Now! Tell me what's in the basket, Brer Rabbit." Mr. Man knowed he had him this time.

Brer Rabbit looked at the basket for a long time, and finally said, "The sparrow can tell you."

Mr. Man like to have fainted. "What kind of creature are you?" he wanted to know. "You must be a hoodoo man." He took the basket out of the tree and there was a gray sparrow inside. He gave Brer Bear another pot of honey and shook his head at Brer Rabbit. "You one of these graveyard rabbits. I'm gon' stay away from you."

After Mr. Man was gone, Brer Bear turned to Brer Rabbit. "Tell me, sho' nuf' Brer Rabbit. How did you know there was a sparrow in there?"

Brer Rabbit laughed. "I didn't. What I said was that only a sparrow could tell, because only a sparrow could fly high enough to see down in the basket."

Brer Rabbit laughed and Brer Bear laughed and they both agreed that the honey was sho' nuf' good.

Brer Wolf, Brer Fox, and the Little Rabbits

Brer Wolf and Brer Fox went to see Brer Rabbit one day. Wasn't nobody home except the little Rabbits playing in the yard. Brer Wolf looked at them. They looked so plump and fat he was licking his chops without knowing he was doing it. Brer Wolf looked at Brer Fox and licked his chops again. Brer Fox looked at Brer Wolf and licked his.

"They mighty fat, ain't they?" said Brer Wolf.

Brer Fox grinned. "Man, hush your mouth!"

The little Rabbits kept on playing but began easing out of the yard. They kept their ears sharp, though.

"Ain't they slick and pretty?" said Brer Wolf.

Brer Fox started drooling. "I wish you'd shut up," he grinned.

The little Rabbits kept playing and inching their way out of the yard and they kept listening.

Brer Wolf smacked his mouth. "Ain't they juicy and tender?"

Brer Fox's eyes started to roll around in his head. "Man, if you don't hush up, I'm going to start twitching, and when I start twitching, I can't help myself."

The little Rabbits kept playing and easing out of the yard and they kept listening.

"Let's eat'em!" Brer Wolf said suddenly!

"Let's eat'em!" exclaimed Brer Fox, twitching all over.

The little Rabbits were still playing, but they knew everything that was going on.

Brer Wolf and Brer Fox decided that when Brer Rabbit got home, one of them would get him in a dispute about something or other and the other one would catch the little Rabbits.

"You best at talking, Brer Wolf. I'll coax the little Rabbits. I got a way with children, you know."

Brer Wolf snorted. "You can't make a gourd out of a pumpkin. You know I ain't never been too good at talking, but your tongue's as slick as glass. I can bite a whole lot better than I can talk. Them little Rabbits don't need coaxing; they need grabbing, and I'm the man for that. You keep Brer Rabbit busy. *I'll* grab the little Rabbits."

They knew that whichever one grabbed the little Rabbits first wasn't gon' leave even a shadow for the other one. While they were arguing back and forth, the little Rabbits took off down the road—*blickety-blickety*—looking for their daddy.

They hadn't gone far when they ran into him coming from town with a jug over his shoulder.

"What you got, Daddy?" they cried.

"A jug of molasses."

"Can we have some?" they wanted to know.

Brer Rabbit pulled the stopper out and let them lick the molasses off the bottom of it. After they'd gotten their breath, they told him all about Brer Fox and Brer Wolf. Brer Rabbit chuckled to himself.

He picked up the jug and he and the little Rabbits started home. When they were almost there, Brer Rabbit said, "Now y'all stay out of sight until I call you."

The little Rabbits were happy to get out of sight, because they had seen Brer Wolf's sharp teeth and Brer Fox's red red tongue. They got down in the weeds and were as still as a mouse in a barrel of flour.

Brer Rabbit sauntered on home. Brer Fox and Brer Wolf were sitting on his front-porch step, smiling smiley smiles. They how-do'd with Brer Rabbit and he how-do'd with them.

"What you got in that jug there, Brer Rabbit?" Brer Wolf wanted to know.

Brer Rabbit hemmed and hawed and made like he didn't want to tell. That made Brer Wolf more curious.

"What you got in that jug, Brer Rabbit?"

Brer Rabbit shook his head and looked real serious. He started talking to Brer Wolf about the weather or whatever and Brer Fox took this chance to sneak off and grab the little Rabbits.

Brer Rabbit unstoppered the jug and handed it to Brer Wolf. "Take a little taste of this."

Brer Wolf took a hit on the jug and smacked his lips. "That's all right, Brer Rabbit! What is it?"

Brer Rabbit leaned close to Brer Wolf. "Don't tell nobody. It's Fox blood."

Brer Wolf's eyes got big. "How you know?"

"I knows what I knows."

"Let me have another hit on that, Brer Rabbit."

Brer Rabbit shook his head. "Don't know how come you want to drink up what little I got when you can get some more for yourself. And the fresher it is, the better."

"How you know?"

"I knows what I knows."

Brer Wolf jumped up and started off after Brer Fox. When he got close, he made a grab for him. Brer Fox ducked and dodged and headed for the woods with Brer Wolf's hot breath on his tail.

When Brer Rabbit got through laughing, he called his young'uns out of the weeds.

Now don't come asking me if Brer Wolf caught Brer Fox. It's all I can do to follow the tale when it's on the big road. Ain't no way I can keep up with them animals when they get to running through the woods. I don't know about you, but when I go in the woods, I got to know where I'm going.

Brer Rabbit's Luck

The time came when the animals made catching Brer Rabbit a full-time job. They didn't even take off holidays or weekends. But no matter what they tried, Brer Rabbit got out of it. They decided Brer Rabbit must have something he conjured with—a John the Conqueror root, a black cat bone, tuna fish casserole, or something!

Brer Bear allowed as to how he thought Brer Rabbit was a natural-born witch. Brer Wolf said he didn't know about that, but it sure wouldn't surprise him if Brer Rabbit was in cahoots with one. Brer Fox said it had to be something like that because Brer Rabbit had more luck than smarts.

That set them to worrying about where Brer Rabbit got his luck when they couldn't buy none with a truckload of money. They worried and fretted so much they couldn't get to sleep at night. Some of them even started getting a little gray over it.

While they were doing all this worrying, one of Brer Bear's children took sick. He asked Miz Rabbit if she would mind setting up a while with Miz Bear to keep her company. Naturally, Miz Rabbit went.

Miz Bear was rocking the baby to keep it from fretting, when all of a sudden Miz Rabbit dropped her knitting. "Oh, my goodness!" she exclaimed.

"What's the matter, Sister Rabbit?"

"I just remembered that I left my ole man's money purse on the mantel. Anybody could walk in and take it. I don't know what he got in there, but whatever it is, he done told me to guard it with my life. What am I going to do, Sister Bear?"

The Tales of Uncle Remus

"Oh, don't worry about it none. I'm sure everything will be all right."

Miz Rabbit said she hoped so, because it was a long way to her house and she wasn't about to go back in the middle of the night.

It just so happened that Brer Wolf was doing his worrying that night on Brer Bear's back porch. He heard every word and took off for Brer Rabbit's.

He sneaked in the house quietly and there on the mantelpiece was Brer Rabbit's purse. Brer Wolf opened it. Inside he found some collard seeds, a calamus root, and a great big rabbit foot! He chuckled and ran home with the purse, as pleased as a man who'd found a gold mine.

Brer Rabbit didn't miss the purse for a few days, but when he did, he tore up the house looking for it. He asked his wife about it. She said she'd given it to him more than a week and a half ago and if he had lost it, don't come blaming her, 'cause it was his purse, and if he didn't have sense enough to keep up with his own things it wasn't her fault, 'cause she had enough to do with taking care of the house and all the children, and speaking of children, when was he going to get them those high-heel sneakers they'd been wanting, 'cause she was tired of hearing about 'em—and Brer Rabbit just sneaked on out.

He was troubled deep in his mind now. "I know where I put that purse, but I don't know where I left it."

All of sudden it seemed like Brer Wolf had all the luck and Brer Rabbit didn't have a lick. Brer Wolf got fat and Brer Rabbit got lean. Brer Wolf could run fast; Brer Rabbit couldn't move as fast as Sister Cow. Brer Wolf felt healthy and Brer Rabbit felt sick all the time. After a month or so, Brer Rabbit knew there was only one thing to do.

He had to talk to Aunt Mammy-Bammy Big-Money.

She was the Witch-Rabbit and lived way off in a deep, dark, dank, smelly, slimey swamp. To get there you had to ride some, slide some; jump some, hump some; hop some, flop some; walk some, balk some; creep some, sleep some; fly some, cry some; follow some, holler some; wade some, spade some; and if you weren't careful, you still wouldn't get there. Brer Rabbit made it, but he was plumb wore out when he did.

He sat down to rest, and in a little while he saw black smoke coming out of a hole in the ground. That was where Aunt Mammy-Bammy Big-Money lived. The smoke got blacker and blacker. Brer Rabbit knew the time had come to say what was on his mind.

"Mammy-Bammy Big-Money, I need your help."

"Son Riley Rabbit, why so? Son Riley Rabbit, why so?"

"Mammy-Bammy Big-Money, I lost that foot you gave me."

"Oh, Riley Rabbit, why so? Son Riley Rabbit, why so?"

"Mammy-Bammy Big Money, my luck done gone. I don't know where that foot is."

"The Wolf took and stole your luck, Son Riley Rabbit, Riley. Go find the track, go get it back, Son Riley Rabbit, Riley."

Aunt Mammy-Bammy Big-Money sucked all the black smoke back in the hole. Brer Rabbit headed for home, wondering how he was going to get the foot back from Brer Wolf. He didn't know, so he hid out near Brer Wolf's house and waited his chance. He waited a day. He waited a week. He waited near 'bout a month.

Finally, one night Brer Wolf came home from a big party. Brer Rabbit knew his waiting was over. After Brer Wolf was good and asleep, Brer Rabbit sneaked in the house. He saw Brer Wolf's coat on the back of a rocking chair. Brer Rabbit searched through the pockets, and in the inside pocket was his purse. He took it and was gone.

Even though he had his purse back and the rabbit's foot was still in it, Brer Rabbit didn't feel like he had his luck back. It seemed that he wasn't getting out of trouble as easily as he used to. Maybe old age was setting in on him.

He decided to go talk things over with Aunt Mammy-Bammy Big-Money again. His wife packed him a lunch of bacon and cornbread.

When he got there, he hollered out, "Mammy-Bammy Big-Money! O Mammy-Bammy Big-Money! I journeyed far, I journeyed fast; I'm glad I found the place at last!"

Great big black smoke rose up out of the ground and Mammy-Bammy Big-Money said, "Where for, Son Riley Rabbit, Riley? Son Riley Rabbit, Riley, where for?"

"Mammy-Bammy Big-Money, I'm afraid I'm losing my mind. Don't seem like I can fool the other animals good as I used to. They done come nigh to catching me here recently and doing away with me for good."

Mammy-Bammy Big-Money sat there sucking in black smoke and belching it out until you couldn't see nothing except her great big eyeballs and her great big ears. Finally, she said, "There's a squirrel up in that tree over yonder, Son Riley. Go catch it and bring it to me, Son Riley Rabbit, Riley."

"I ain't got much sense left," Brer Rabbit said, "but if I can't get that squirrel out of that tree, I'm in worse shape than I thought I was."

Brer Rabbit went over to the tree, took the bacon and cornbread out of the bag, found two rocks, and put the bag over his hands. He waited a little while, then he banged the two rocks together—*blip!*

Squirrel hollered, "Hey!"

Brer Rabbit waited a little longer and then slapped the rocks together again—*blap!*

Squirrel ran down the tree a little ways and hollered, "Heyo!"

Brer Rabbit don't say a word, but pops the rocks together—*blop!*

Squirrel came down the tree trunk a little bit farther. "Who that?"

"Biggidy Dicky Big-Bag," said Brer Rabbit.

"What you doing?"

"Cracking hickory nuts."

"Can I crack some?"

"Come get in the bag," Brer Rabbit said.

Squirrel hesitated, then scampered down the tree and right into the bag. Brer Rabbit closed it tight, tied it, and gave it to Mammy-Bammy Big-Money.

The ole Witch-Rabbit turned the squirrel loose and said, "There's a snake lying over there in the grass, Son Riley. Bring him here and be fast about it, Son Riley Rabbit, Riley."

Brer Rabbit looked around and saw the biggest rattlesnake he'd ever seen. He was wrapped around himself five or six times and looked like he was ready to do business with anybody come down the pike.

Brer Rabbit studied the situation for a few minutes, then went off in the bushes, cut a young grapevine, and made a slipknot in it.

"How you today, Mr. Snake?"

Snake don't say a word. He just coiled up a little tighter,

flicking his tongue in and out of his mouth quicker than a lamb can shake its tail.

Brer Rabbit don't pay it no never mind. "I'm glad I ran into you today. Me and Brer Bear was arguing a few weeks ago about how long you are. We both agree that you the prettiest thing ever swished across the earth. You even prettier when you curled up in the sun like you are now. Brer Bear say that when you stretch out you about three feet long. I told him he better get his eyes examined, 'cause I know you five feet long if you an inch. Well, we got to arguing back and forth so much, I come close to going upside Brer Bear's head with my walking stick."

Mr. Snake don't say a word, but seemed to relax a little bit.

"I told Brer Bear that the next time I saw you I was going to take your measurements. So that's why I'm glad I run into you today. Would you be so good as to uncoil yourself?"

Mr. Snake was feeling mighty proud now, and he stretched himself out like he was being judged in a contest.

"That's one foot," Brer Rabbit said, as he started measuring from the tail forward. "Two feet. There's Brer Bear's three feet and I still got a ways to go. Four feet."

Brer Rabbit was at the head now and just as he said, "Five feet! That's what I told Brer Bear," he dropped the slipknot over Mr. Snake's head and pulled it tight. He dragged the Snake over to Mammy-Bammy Big-Money, but when he got there, she had disappeared.

Then he heard a voice from far off: "If you get any more sense, Son Riley, you gon' be the death of us all, Son Riley Rabbit, Riley."

Brer Rabbit felt all right now. He took the snake home, made snake stew, and used the snake oil as an ointment for his limbs. He didn't need no oil for his brain. Fact was, Brer Rabbit thought he just might be better than ever.

Julius Lester is the critically acclaimed author of books for both children and adults. His six Dial books include *To Be a Slave*, the first Newbery Medal Honor Book by a black author; *Long Journey Home: Stories from Black History*, a National Book Award finalist; *Who I Am; Two Love Stories; This Strange New Feeling*; and *The Knee-High Man and Other Tales*, an American Library Association Notable Book and Lewis Carroll Shelf Award Winner. His adult books include *Search for the New Land; The Seventh Son: The Thought and Writings of W.E.B. Du Bois*; and *Do Lord Remember Me*. The son of a Methodist minister, Mr. Lester was born in St. Louis. At fourteen he moved to Nashville, where he was later to receive his Bachelor of Arts from Fisk University. The father of four children, Mr. Lester now lives in Amherst, where he teaches at the University of Massachusetts.

Jerry Pinkney received the Coretta Scott King Award for Illustration and the Christopher Award for his latest book for Dial, *The Patchwork Quilt*, written by Valerie Flournoy. Mr. Pinkney's artwork has been shown at the 1986 International Children's Book Exhibition at the Bologna Book Fair and in museums around the country. He studied at the Philadelphia Museum College of Art. He and his wife, who have four grown children, live in Croton-on-Hudson, New York.

OTHER PUFFIN BOOKS YOU MAY ENJOY

Charlie Pippin   Candy Dawson Boyd

Chevrolet Saturdays   Candy Dawson Boyd

Fast Sam, Cool Clyde, and Stuff   Walter Dean Myers

Freedom Songs   Yvette Moore

The Friendship   Mildred D. Taylor

The Gold Cadillac   Mildred D. Taylor

The Hundred Penny Box   Sharon Bell Mathis

Let the Circle Be Unbroken   Mildred D. Taylor

Like Sisters on the Homefront   Rita Williams-Garcia

Long Journey Home   Julius Lester

My Black Me   Arnold Adoff, editor

My Life with Martin Luther King, Jr.   Coretta Scott King

The Road to Memphis   Mildred D. Taylor

Roll of Thunder, Hear My Cry   Mildred D. Taylor

Sidewalk Story   Sharon Bell Mathis

Soul Looks Back in Wonder   Tom Feelings

The Well   Mildred D. Taylor

Won't Know Till I Get There   Walter Dean Myers

The Young Landlords   Walter Dean Myers